P9-CSH-235

Because
She's My
Friend

Because She's My Friend

Harriet Sirof

Atheneum   1993   *New York*

MAXWELL MACMILLAN CANADA
Toronto
MAXWELL MACMILLAN INTERNATIONAL
New York   Oxford   Singapore   Sydney

Atheneum
Macmillan Publishing Company
866 Third Avenue
New York, NY 10022

Maxwell Macmillan Canada, Inc.
1200 Eglinton Avenue East
Suite 200
Don Mills, Ontario M3C 3N1

Macmillan Publishing Company is part of the Maxwell Communication
Group of Companies.

First edition
Printed in the United States of America
10   9   8   7   6   5   4   3   2   1
The text of this book is set in 11 point Caledonia.

Library of Congress Cataloging-in-Publication Data

Sirof, Harriet.
Because she's my friend / Harriet Sirof. — 1st ed.
p.   cm.
Summary: Mutual need creates an intense, difficult friendship between
fourteen-year-old Teri, the well-behaved "baby" of an extended
Italian-American family, and spoiled Valerie, who has one leg paralyzed
from a freak accident.
ISBN 0-689-31844-8
[1. Friendship—Fiction.   2. Physically handicapped—Fiction.
3. Italian Americans—Fiction.]   I. Title.
PZ7.S6217Be   1993
[Fic]—dc20   92-46426

For Sid, my best friend

Because She's My Friend

1

Teresa D'Angelo

~

*T*he hospital smelled like somebody threw up and they used too much disinfectant on the mop cleaning it up. Rosanne didn't mention the smell when she talked me into being a junior volunteer.

Rosanne takes being my older sister very seriously. She's always after me to go out and do things where I'll meet people. She says I need more get-up-and-go, and I say she has plenty for both of us, but she can out-argue me anytime and I usually end up doing whatever it is.

She came up with the hospital volunteer idea while she was packing for her summer job waitressing at this hotel in the mountains. With tips, she figured she'd make enough to pay her nursing school tuition next fall. I'd begged Papa to let me go with her, but he wouldn't hear of it. He didn't care that he was dooming me to a whole summer of sitting in our bedroom staring at Rosanne's empty bed and biting my fingernails.

I complained to Rosanne, "It's not fair. Just because

you're going to college, Papa treats you like a grown-up and me like a baby. He doesn't understand I'm practically fifteen."

"Not for three more months. And you won't be the baby anymore after October."

"Great." Like I wasn't miserable enough without being reminded of Mama's big belly. At her age. I'm ashamed to be seen in the street with her even though we just moved in and nobody around here knows me. And if it wasn't for the baby coming, we'd still be on Broome Street where I'd lived all my life. But Mama decided we needed more room, and Papa's cousin—who's the super of this building—finagled us an apartment and we moved uptown, miles away from everybody I know. I feel like Saint Jerome in the desert.

Rosanne folded a blouse carefully. "Teri, you can't mope around all by yourself all summer."

"Maybe Papa'll hire me at the garage."

She didn't bother telling me not to be silly. "Did you try for Mama's old checker's job at the supermarket?"

"They said too bad Mama didn't tell them I wanted the job when she quit, but I was first on the list for the next opening."

She tucked the blouse neatly into her suitcase. Rosanne was born neat. At least while she was away I could drop my stuff on the floor without getting a lecture. She said, "You should be a hospital volunteer until the supermarket job opens up. Besides helping people, it counts as Christian Service for school. I did it when I was your age, and I loved it."

I let Rosanne talk me into it because I'd have a miserable summer either way, so I might as well do something for other people. Now I found myself wandering all over Saint Cosmas Hospital looking for the volunteer office.

Rosanne'd made me a map with the office marked with an X. I should've known better than to follow it. I'm the one with the sense of direction. But she acted so sure and the map was so neat that I figured it had to be right.

It wasn't. I trudged through endless hospital corridors, turning left and right with no idea where I was going, hoping sooner or later I'd stumble onto the volunteer office. I didn't have the nerve to stop anyone for directions. Everyone I passed was rushing like they were on life-or-death errands.

Finally I came to a door marked P.T. A gym. It was either ask in there or wander for the rest of my life. I stuck my head in.

A man in gym shorts was doing sit-ups on a mat near the door while a woman in a white jacket held his legs. I cleared my throat. "Excuse me . . ." Then it hit me that one of the man's legs wasn't real. It wore a sneaker just like the other leg, but it was made of pinkish plastic. My tongue got tangled up in my mouth.

The woman turned to me with her hand still on the false leg. "Yes?"

I stammered that I was looking for the volunteer office.

She smiled. How could she smile holding that terrible thing? "Go back to the . . . Wait. John is finished. He can show you on his way out."

John was a young man on crutches. He was wearing jeans so I couldn't tell if both legs were his. And I didn't want to know. He swung down the corridor, and I followed him to a door marked Mrs. McKay, Director of Volunteers. It was to the right of the main entrance, not to the

3

left like on Rosanne's map. I thanked him and ducked inside.

Mrs. McKay was at her desk. "Can I help you, dear?"

"I'm Teresa D'Angelo. Rosanne's sister."

"Rosanne called to say you were coming. Rosanne was one of my most dedicated volunteers and now I'm delighted to have her sister." She explained about uniforms and signing in and out and a lunch ticket if I worked a full day. She warned me never to read patients' charts or accept tips. She gave me a form to fill out and a manual to read. Then she asked, "Shall we try you on the candy cart? It's really a two-person job, although Henrietta has been managing by herself. Henrietta volunteers five days a week."

Feeling that I was letting Mrs. McKay and Rosanne and Henrietta and all the other dedicated people down, I said the candy cart was fine but maybe I should just do two days a week to start.

Half an hour later, I was wearing a red-and-white-striped apron and pushing a cart of snacks, games, and things from room to room while Henrietta sold the stuff to the patients. Henrietta was a tiny old lady with blue-rinsed hair and big, green rhinestone earrings. She told me proudly that she was eighty-one years old. She looked a hundred and eighty-one, but she had an eagle eye and a memory like a computer. She had something to say about every sale and no-sale, about every passing nurse and doctor, about the way the volunteer program and the hospital in general were run. I was sure things would run a lot better if they put Henrietta in charge.

We stopped outside room 725. Henrietta took a choc-

4

olate bar, a *Seventeen* magazine, and a jigsaw puzzle off the cart. "Take these in. And don't come right out."

Until then, I'd stood in the doorways with the cart while she went into the rooms to ask if the patients wanted anything. Which was all right with me. I didn't much like seeing the oxygen masks and tubes and things. How can Rosanne want to be a nurse and look at that stuff all the time? As I hesitated, Henrietta gave me a push. "It's a girl your age. Go visit."

One of the two beds in the room was empty. The girl in the other bed was lying with her back to the door and the sheet pulled up so all you could see was her hair. She had the Michelle Pfeiffer kind of blond hair that I'd give my eyeteeth for. My hair is dark and frizzes up when it rains. The nameplate over her bed read: Valerie Ross.

I walked over to the bed, but Valerie didn't move. I stood there. If she was sleeping, I didn't want to wake her. But maybe she'd asked specially for the stuff I was carrying. Should I put it on her table?

The blond head came up. Two emerald-green eyes stared at me. Why can't *I* have eyes like that? I wondered why she was in the hospital. I asked, "Did you want the new *Seventeen*?"

"Get out."

Her voice was so calm that the words didn't register. I asked, "Or this jigsaw puzzle?"

She told me exactly where to put the magazine and puzzle, pronouncing each word clearly in a snobby public-TV voice so I wouldn't miss a single syllable. Then she fastened those green eyes on me like a snake staring at a mouse, challenging me to do or say something.

5

I just stood there like a statue of a saint in church. I'd come in specially to be nice to her and out of the blue . . .

When I couldn't find my voice, she shrugged and turned her head away. Like I wasn't worth bothering with. Like I wasn't even in the room.

That upset me more than the nasty things she'd said. If you curse at someone, at least you admit they exist. Ignoring someone is the most hurtful thing you can do. In my hurt I blurted out, "You're horrible. You deserve to be sick. I don't care if you never get better." And I ran out of the room.

The guilt hit me halfway down the hall. How could I have said such a terrible thing to a sick person? I never did anything like that before. Ask my family; they'll tell you it's not like me. I immediately swore to the Holy Mother that I didn't mean it.

I caught up with Henrietta, who was selling perfume to a woman in a pink robe who had to sniff every bottle before she decided. When the woman finally made up her mind, there was a whole business about paying for it. The woman wanted to change a fifty-dollar bill. Henrietta refused to take anything larger than a twenty. Valerie could've died before they settled it.

At last the woman pocketed her change and I was able to ask Henrietta, "The girl in seven twenty-five. What's wrong with her?"

Henrietta shook her head sadly. "Poor thing. She had an accident that left her right leg paralyzed. One of our best surgeons operated on her. It didn't do any good. They say there may be improvement in time, but I have my doubts."

Sweet Mary, what had I done? I ran back to Valerie's

room like the devil was chasing me, ignoring Henrietta's calling after me. I had to apologize. I had to make it right.

Valerie had the sheet pulled up again. It hid all of her except her hair. I said, loud enough for her to hear through the sheet, "I'm sorry. I didn't mean what I said. I hope you get well real fast."

She didn't answer, but the sheet came down. When I saw her eyes, I felt so awful that I'd have donated one of my legs to her if there was such a thing as a leg transplant. I said, "I'm sorry I made you cry."

"*You* make me cry? Don't flatter yourself."

"Your eyes are all red . . ."

"Allergy. Even a stupid candy cane must have heard of allergies."

I couldn't help smiling at the "candy cane." That was exactly what had popped into my head when I saw my reflection in the locker room mirror.

"Stop grinning like an effing idiot. Don't you have the brains to know when you're being insulted?" She let loose with another string of insults.

I stood there and let them bounce off me. I wish I could say it was because Sister Josephine's lectures in school on the good Christian life taught me patience and forbearance. The truth is: I let Valerie insult me because I was *standing*. On two good legs. Because it gave me the shivers just to imagine being paralyzed and never running or walking again. If a horrible thing like that happened to me, I'd curl up and die.

Besides, I'd never met a girl who cursed like Valerie. It was interesting to see how far she'd go.

She went pretty far. It got more and more interesting. It almost seemed a shame to stop her, but I broke in, "I

7

came back to apologize for being mean to you. Even though you started it. So I'm saying I'm sorry and I hope you get better soon, but I don't have to let you curse me out all day."

"Isn't that part of your Florence-Nightingale-Mother-Teresa-be-kind-to-cripples act?"

I had the funny feeling she was playing some kind of game with me—a game I didn't know the rules to. I'm not very good at games. I feel stupid when I lose and guilty if I win. So I just said, "I couldn't be like Mother Teresa if I tried for a million years. I couldn't dedicate my life to the poor and the sick. I'm only a junior volunteer and today is my first day and Henrietta told me to visit you."

"Sit."

"What?"

"If you came to visit, don't just stand there like a fire hydrant. Sit down."

I sat on the chair near the bed. Valerie pointed to a fancy tin box on her table. "Have a toffee. My grandmother sent them from England."

I took a toffee. She reached for the box and winced. I moved it toward her. She threw me a fierce look, pushed the box back to where it was, then got it for herself. "I'm not a bleeding cripple. Just remember that."

We chewed our toffee in silence for a while. Then, even though I'm not good at making conversation, I figured it was up to me to try. "Does your grandmother live in England?"

She took so long to answer that I almost gave up. At last, "In London. I usually spend July there with her."

"Really? Did you ever see Princess Di? Or Fergie?"

8

"Actually, we're distantly related to one of King Edward the Seventh's mistresses. You know, the Jersey Lily."

I didn't know, and Valerie turned out to be one of those people who likes telling you what they know. She told me all about this ancestor of hers, Lillie Langtry, who was the most beautiful woman in England a hundred years ago. She described how her great-grand-aunt a few times removed toured the world with her own acting company and was the toast of Europe.

I had never met anyone before with royalty in her family, and Valerie told it so well that I practically saw the theaters and castles and heard the music and smelled the perfume. I said, "That's a great story. You should write it down."

"I'm not interested in doing biography. I write fiction."

I was impressed. It's a mystery to me how people can write stories. When I have to write an essay for school, I do okay with the introduction and the body, but I can never think of a good conclusion. I said as much.

"What *can* you do?"

"I can fix a car engine." I can do basic maintenance and a lot of minor repairs. If I were a boy, Papa'd give me a summer job in the garage in a minute.

Valerie wasn't impressed. "Are you good at math?"

I nodded.

She considered. "Mechanics and math." Then she handed down her decision. "Study engineering. M.I.T.'s the best, but City has a good program too." Then, having disposed of my whole life in two seconds, she lost interest. She slid down in bed and closed her eyes. Who did she think she was? The queen of England?

I said, "I better go. Henrietta'll be throwing fits."

9

"Go." She turned away and pulled up the sheet. Then she peeked out. "Leave the jigsaw."

I surprised myself by offering, "I'll come back tomorrow and do it with you." I hadn't planned to volunteer tomorrow.

"Suit yourself." Her voice was muffled by the sheet.

I told myself I had nothing better to do tomorrow and seeing how Valerie would act next was more interesting than cleaning out my side of our clothes closet like Rosanne said I'd better do this summer or else. The truth is: It bothered me to leave Valerie lying there all alone under her sheet like she didn't have a friend in the world. I said, "It's a hard puzzle, but we'll manage it together."

2

Valerie Ross

I had as much privacy in the effing hospital as I would being chained naked under the clock in Grand Central Station. People paraded through without so much as a "May I?". Nurses for temperature and blood pressure, technicians wanting blood, aides to make the bed, men to polish the floor, people with trays of the garbage they call food, and What's-her-face.

I was stuck in the effing bed right in the middle of the parade route. I couldn't even go to the bathroom because the nurses insisted the leg wouldn't hold me. The nurses were dead wrong. The surgeon told Amanda there was a 90 percent chance of the operation working, a 90 percent chance of walking normally again. He should know; he operated on a top-seeded tennis player who's winning at Wimbledon again.

The only reason I still couldn't move the leg was because it was so swollen. Which was to be expected because it was only a week since the operation. Or was it eight days?

My watch calendar said 7/6 and I came in on the . . .

Who cares what day it is. Or what time. I didn't care that afternoon visiting hours had started. I wasn't expecting any visitors. Amanda took time off from work for my operation, but a woman trying to make it in a man's world can't afford the luxury of absence for every family crisis. So she comes at night. Actually, most nights she has to work so late that she barely has time to ask how I'm feeling, tell me I'm looking better, and give me the present she's brought before the nurses start shooing her out.

Actually, I'm just as glad Amanda doesn't have more time to visit. I don't want to hear about the African violet in the kitchen blooming or her getting an order from Zambia at work. She doesn't understand that nothing but the hospital exists for me, that I can't believe there's still a world outside where the sun shines on flowers and people stroll in the open air.

I'm trying to remember what Amanda and I talked about before the accident. Actually, we didn't talk much, although it was just the two of us in the apartment after she divorced Dad. That's strange when you think about it, because we get along better than most mothers and daughters. I love Amanda and I'm sure she loves me, but you're not always close to people you love. Not if closeness means confiding your fears and sharing your dreams. We're both always too busy. Amanda brings work home from the office and I have studying. We never seem to have time for what Gran calls "a proper heart-to-heart."

Dad promised to come to the hospital when Amanda couldn't. He said it was better if they took turns. (Translation: He's uncomfortable being in the same room with

Amanda since he took up with a girl young enough to be my sister.) Dad's turn worked out to one quick pop-in on his lunch hour.

And Gran is in England. She'd be on the first plane out of Heathrow if she wasn't forbidden to fly because of her heart. Gran called right after the operation when I was too drugged to do more than mumble. I wish she'd waited until now so I could tell her how much I hate this place.

My other grandparents (Dad's folks) moved to Florida and never come north. And I certainly wasn't holding my breath for some friend to show up. Kids are embarrassed by sickness or afraid it'll rub off on them like a dog's fleas. So they avoid you. Which is fine with me. I can't bear people feeling sorry for me. Two girls from school visited me after the accident and nattered about how awful it was until I got so mad I told them to take the disgusting candy they brought and stuff it.

So, for all I care, they can cancel afternoon visiting hours permanently for lack of interest. They can cancel the whole effing day. The week. Month. Year.

I turned on my side and pulled the sheet up over my head. Turning sent pain shooting out from where they'd cut into me. I scrunched into a ball to make myself hurt more. Pain shuts everything else out. I hid under the sheet with the hurt.

Footsteps, and I felt someone standing near my bed. Probably the candy cane dithering over whether to wake me. That girl has the backbone of a worm. Taking pity on her, I moved to show I was awake. Ouch!

Amanda's voice asked, "Valerie, are you in pain?"

Amanda? What was she doing here in the afternoon? I opened my eyes. Dad was standing next to her.

13

I knew immediately. I didn't want to know. I didn't want to hear. When their mouths moved, I tried to close my ears to the buildup about my being grown-up and strong enough to face the situation. I refused to hear them say that the surgeon was disappointed because yesterday's tests showed so much nerve damage, and while that didn't mean I wouldn't ever be able to walk again, the odds were no longer in my favor.

I started to scream. No words. No thoughts, even. Just noise pouring out of me to block out their voices, to block everything out.

I was screaming so hard that I barely felt the jab of the needle. Dad held my hand and Amanda stroked my hair. After a while the screaming stopped.

When I woke up, I thought I was in my bedroom at home. Except someone had moved everything while I was sleeping. The window was in the wrong place and the walls were the wrong color and my posters and rocking chair were missing.

Then it all came flooding back. I was in the hospital and Amanda and Dad had come together to bring me the bad news.

Where were they? I looked frantically around the room as if they were playing hide-and-seek and I'd find them behind the curtain or in the closet. Nobody was there. I never felt so alone in my life.

Hearing the tap of footsteps in the hall, I went weak with relief. They'd just gone out for a "cuppa" and were coming back to take care of me.

Then the footsteps went past. I looked at my watch. I'd slept for hours. Amanda and Dad had important jobs; I couldn't expect them to sit all afternoon watching me sleep.

I turned my back on the door my parents weren't coming through and stared out the window. If I lifted my head, I could see people walking down the street. I'd never walk down the street again. I wanted to throw myself out the window and smash myself into oblivion on the hard pavement. I closed my eyes and burrowed my head into the pillow.

A voice whispered, "Are you sleeping?"

I opened my eyes. The candy cane was standing by my bed. For the first time I understood why, when you see people being rescued from some catastrophe on the evening news, they throw their arms around complete strangers. I said, "I'm awake."

"I peeked in a couple of times before, but you were always sleeping."

"Or screaming."

She looked embarrassed. I expected her to scuttle out like a startled cockroach, but she stood her ground. "Want to talk about it?"

Normally, I keep my feelings to myself. I write them in my journal or make them into a story. In my weakened condition, I couldn't help myself. The dam broke and the words poured out, "My mother and father were here together. They'd never come together if it weren't hopeless. They said the doctor told them I might get some return, that it happens in a lot of cases, but that was just to make me feel better. So I wouldn't make a fuss. Amanda hates fusses. She gave me the things-will-get-better bit and Dad kept nodding yes-yes. But I wouldn't buy it. I couldn't buy it. I made the fuss of the age. I screamed the house down. Because things won't get better. I won't get better. I'll never walk again. I'll be an effing cripple sitting in an

15

effing wheelchair with the whole effing world feeling sorry for me. I was going to be a writer. Jane Austen, Charlotte Brontë, move over. Now I'll be lucky to peddle pencils on a street corner."

Her concerned expression made me think she understood. Until she said, "You can still be a writer. Writers work with their heads, not with their feet."

It was exactly the kind of effing cheer-up answer you'd expect from Ms. Do-good. It was my own fault for talking to her, for acting like some old lady on the bus who dumps her life story on the first person who sits near her. But I'd blamed myself for enough already. I'd blamed myself every day since the accident for not waiting for the super to hang my new mobile, for piling books on the step stool to do it myself, for falling. There is only so much blame a person can take on herself. Then it's someone else's turn. I picked up my water pitcher and heaved it at the candy cane's earnest face.

A sharp stab of pain checked my throw. The pitcher hit the footboard of the bed and poured icy water all over my feet. And there was nothing I could do to help myself. I couldn't bend forward to pull the wet sheet off. I couldn't even move my bad leg out of the puddle.

She went into her hospital-helper routine. (I bet she wouldn't have been so helpful if I'd hit her.) She mopped up the puddle with my towel and put one of those blue-paper waterproof things over it. She took off the wet top sheet and dried my feet. She never gave a thought to the miracle of her own body obeying her.

While she worked she told me, "My sister, Rosanne, is training to be a nurse. She says nurses like good patients, the ones who behave and don't complain and are always

16

cheerful. But the bad patients get well faster. Rosanne says that's because bad patients are fighters. They fight everyone and everything, but they fight their sickness too. And they get well." She dropped the sopping towel into the bin. "You're probably the worst patient in this hospital."

I stared at her. That was the first sensible thing anyone had said to me in this place: If you want to get well, fight, kick, scream. Who'd have thought she had it in her? "According to your brilliant sister, the nerves in my leg should be working in no time."

"That's not what Rosanne meant. She meant . . ." Then she caught on; she wasn't as dumb as she looked. "You're being difficult on purpose."

I complained, "You did a rotten job of drying this bed."

"That's because you did such a good job of drenching it."

Would wonders never cease? The girl had some spirit after all. "I need clean sheets. Ring for the nurse. Although they don't exactly come running because I'm . . ."

We finished the sentence together: ". . . a bad patient."

The injection they'd given me began to make me woozy again. My eyes closed while we waited.

I forced them open. She was sitting patiently by my bed. I said, "You never told me your name."

"Teresa D'Angelo. My friends call me Teri."

"I'm Valerie Ross."

"I know. It's on the nameplate on your wall."

"Wonderful. I'd have more privacy in a goldfish bowl. But just try to get a nurse when I need one."

"I'll go see if I can find someone."

I called after her, "Teri. Thanks."

17

3

Teri

❦

*T*he kitchen was so hot that I felt like I was baking along with the lasagna in the oven. Mama had all four stove burners going. Pots of minestrone soup, chicken Cacciatore, and veal with peppers bubbled on three of them. She was frying zucchini in a pan over the fourth.

I never minded the heat before this summer. When I complained I was melting, Mama said my body couldn't get used to the weather because I spent five days a week in the hospital's air conditioning. Valerie would've answered that bending over a hot iron wasn't helping any. But back talk isn't my style. Lifting the company tablecloth off the ironing board, I said, "The iron cord is loose. I'll fix it when it cools."

I spread the cloth on the big folding table we set up in the living room when the family comes to dinner. Mama cooks dinner for the whole family every fourth Sunday.

Aunt Paula, Aunt Flo, and Aunt Sophie take their turns the other Sundays.

Papa was sitting on the couch reading the Sunday *News* with the fan blowing on him. Mama says that's a sure way to catch cold. I'd happily risk a cold to plop down in front of the fan, but, with Rosanne away, Mama only had me to help her. I went back to the kitchen.

Mama was stirring the soup on the back burner with her belly pressed against the stove. Sweat was dripping down her face. It bothered me to look at her. Valerie says the reason Mama's belly bothers me is because it proves Mama and Papa still . . . you know. She says if Rosanne were married and having a baby, I'd be thrilled to pieces. Maybe she's right, but I'd like to see how unbothered she'd be if her mother looked like a dripping-wet beach ball.

I took the spoon out of Mama's hand. "I'll do that. You rest a little." She surprised me by sitting down. Mama never sits still. She's always cooking or cleaning or washing or mending. I suggested, "Next time the family comes you should buy some of the food. Valerie says her mother buys lasagna and ravioli and stuff in this store on Ninety-eighth Street."

"Store-bought lasagna. Cardboard smeared with ketchup."

"Valerie says it's practically homemade. The Italian couple who own the store do their own cooking. I know it won't be as good as yours, but at least try it."

Mama said, "We'll see" in the tone that means, "Over my dead body." She struggled to her feet and opened the oven to check her homemade lasagna. "Lately every other word out of your mouth is 'Valerie says.' What is your new friend like?"

It was strange that she had to ask—and fun. Before we moved, I palled around with Julia and Patsy on our block, and Mama had known them since they were babies. I could just imagine her face if I told her that Valerie cursed and threw tantrums and talked about our right to oppose authority and that I thought she was wonderful.

I said, "Valerie is half-Jewish and half-English, but on the hospital forms she's American and Protestant because she was born here and it goes by the mother's religion. Her father met her mother when he worked in his company's English office, and they got married. They're divorced now, but they still work for the same company here in New York, only on different floors. Valerie lives with her mother on Central Park West not very far from here. Valerie is very smart. She goes to Hunter High, and you have to be practically a genius to get in there. She wants to be a writer and her teachers say she has talent."

Mama nodded. "I see why her mother serves store-bought lasagna. A divorced woman has to work all day and then come home to do the housework and be both mother and father to her child. You bring Valerie to Sunday dinner when she's better, and I'll show her what real food tastes like."

Mama isn't happy unless she's feeding the whole world. And she's a terrific cook. So why did I wish she hadn't thought of inviting Valerie? "She might never get better. She might be in a wheelchair the rest of her life."

"Poor child! What happened?"

"She was doing her room over and fell off a ladder and paralyzed her leg."

"How dreadful to be struck down so young." Mama's eyes filled with tears. She's terribly softhearted. Whenever somebody's in trouble, she's the first one running to help.

I tried to make her feel better. "You should see Valerie scoot around in that wheelchair like it's a sports car. She goes like the wind. She's not afraid of anything."

"Teresa, you're a good girl. I'm proud you made friends with a crippled girl."

"Mama, it's not nice to say 'crippled.' In the hospital they say 'disabled.' Anyway, I don't care about Valerie's disability. I *want* to be her friend." The problem was, did Valerie want to be my friend? Sure, while she was stuck in the hospital and I was the only one around. But what about after?

Mama smiled. "It's even better when it comes from the heart. Now let's see. The wheelchair can go down the baby carriage ramp to the basement and then up the elevator . . ."

I was relieved when the doorbell interrupted her. I ran to answer it. It was Aunt Flo and Uncle Charley carrying a big bakery box. Aunt Flo's hair was freshly bleached, teased, and sprayed into place—just like a woman Valerie and I passed in the hospital corridor Friday. Valerie had nudged me and whispered that the woman's hair was made of yellow-painted plaster to save combing and washing, and we both giggled. Now Aunt Flo was standing there with the same hairdo. I never noticed before how awful it looks.

I gave her a specially big kiss because I felt so guilty. Aunt Flo is the nicest of my aunts. It's like her to come early to help Mama and to bring a big box of can-

21

noli besides. So what if Valerie would sneer at her hair?

I felt guilty all day because I kept seeing the family through Valerie's eyes. I imagined Valerie turning her nose up at Uncle Charley's chewed-on cigar, Aunt Paula's black mourning dress, and the grease Papa can never get out from under his fingernails even though he's manager of the garage now. The only one I could've shown off to Valerie was my cousin Marco. I mean Marc; he hates being called Marco. Marc looks like Robert DeNiro, dresses like he stepped out of a Guess ad, and drives a red sports car. But Marc hadn't come today, so I was left watching Uncle Charley pick pieces of veal out of his teeth.

I wished Mama hadn't started in on inviting Valerie to Sunday dinner. Now I was imagining her sitting at the table with Sister Josephine's grading book, giving my family demerits for eating too much and talking too loud. And I was entering my demerits in the book next to Valerie's.

As I sat there giving my family bad marks for not being clever or elegant, I felt like I was committing some kind of sin. I couldn't put a name on my sin. It wasn't stealing or bearing false witness or worshipping idols. It wasn't gluttony or sloth or envy. But I knew for sure it was a sin.

The next day, Valerie was in the hall in her wheelchair when I stepped out of the elevator. She came at me like a taxi trying to beat the light and screeched to a stop inches short of the closing door. She scared me into saying, "Careful. You'll get hurt."

"Want to see me do wheelies?"

If I said no, she'd do them on purpose to upset me.

22

"Later. My mother sent you this." I dropped a cake box in her lap. "Mama thinks anybody in a hospital is starving to death. She wanted to send chicken Cacciatore, but I refused to lug a thermos back and forth so she settled for two cannoli. My Aunt Flo buys them in this great bakery on Mulberry Street."

Valerie tore open the box and bit a big hunk off one of the pastries, scattering creamy crumbs into her lap. Mama was right about people in hospitals starving for real food. After she devoured both cannoli and licked her fingers, Valerie announced, "I'm going home the day after to-morrow. They're fitting me for a leg brace tomorrow and letting me out Wednesday."

For a second I stood there with my mouth open like I expected her to stick a cannoli into it. Then I made myself say, "That's great! I bet you can't wait to get home."

" 'Tis a consummation devoutly to be wished. Translation for the ignorant: When I shake off the dust of this effing place, I'm never coming within a mile of anyone or anything to do with it."

"Won't you miss anyone? I mean, there's that young nurse who shampooed your hair . . ."

I trailed off because Valerie was staring at me like I'd just flipped out. Which I had. I had to be out of my mind to fish around for Valerie to say that naturally she didn't mean me, and of course she wanted to keep being my friend after she got home, and why didn't I come around one afternoon soon to do the thousand-piece jigsaw puzzle with the picture of Big Ben her grandmother sent from England. A person in her right mind would just invite herself over to work on the puzzle.

23

I didn't invite myself. I gathered up the cake box and wrappings. Mama always packs things like she's sending them to China. Then I went to dump them.

When I came back, Valerie was doing sharp turns in her wheelchair. Watching her gave me a funny feeling deep in my stomach, like leaning out too far while washing windows.

I never should've let the feeling show. Valerie gave me a big grin. "Look what I can do."

I don't know what she meant to do. I just know that when she suddenly tipped her wheelchair back I was sure she was going to fall. I screamed.

She looked startled. The chair hung balanced on its rear wheels for a long moment and then toppled over backward. Her head hit the wall with a sickening crack.

The wheelchair lay on its side. Valerie lay still, half in and half out of the chair.

I ran to pick her up. Just in time, I remembered that you never move an accident victim. I turned and ran toward the nurses' station, running faster than I ever ran in my life, crying, "Nurse! Help!" and praying, "Dear God, don't let her be dead."

4

Valerie

———

I was flat on my back in bed. They'd forbidden everything: no wheelchair, no bathroom, no turning on my
stomach (as if I could). I'd been lying here like a sack
of soggy laundry for days. Until this morning, although I
made grumbling sounds to keep up my reputation, I was
glad not to move. Two little men with hammers pounded
inside my skull while waves of dizziness and nausea
washed over me.

The nurses said I'd given myself a slight concussion
when I banged my head as my wheelchair toppled over.
Slight! If I had the energy, I'd sick up all over the floor
to show them how slight it was.

Actually, I didn't much feel like vomiting anymore. My
stomach had settled down. And (thank goodness!) my mind
was clear again. Yesterday (or was it the day before?) I
kept sliding into a strange sleep. Each time I fell asleep,
I found myself back in the same horrible dream—as if I'd
slipped through a time warp into another universe. The

dream was so real that I was totally convinced it was really happening until I woke up crying. Then I couldn't remember the dream at all. But I couldn't stop crying either.

Which shows how serious the concussion was. I never cry. When Amanda told me she was divorcing Dad because he'd taken up with a twenty-three-year-old tart, my eyes were as dry as the Sahara Desert. I said I'd known for a long time that things weren't right between them. I said, "You and Dad were too polite to each other, as if you didn't care enough to fight." Then I went into my room and wrote a story about a man who betrays his daughter and she kills him.

Even the pain after the operation didn't make me cry. The private nurse I had the first nights urged me to "Let loose, dearie. It's all right to cry." But I just gritted my teeth until she gave me another shot.

Now I was sick of being flat on my back. I rang for the nurse, jabbing the button again and again although I knew the light went on outside my room the first time. When the nurse finally arrived, I demanded to be let out of bed immediately.

"Dr. Lucas will be in to see you this afternoon. He'll decide if you can get up."

I made a fuss on principle, insisting that I didn't know any Dr. Lucas, that he wasn't my doctor, that I wanted out right now. It didn't help. Nurses aren't allowed to breathe unless a doctor writes a prescription for air.

Tired of waiting for Dr. Whoosis, I picked up the phone. And dropped it because there was nobody to call. Amanda can't talk long at work. She'd ask was anything wrong or did I need something. When I said no, she'd promise to try to come early tonight and hang up. Dad would be in

26

a meeting. I even considered calling Gran, but hospitals don't permit overseas calls from patients' phones.

Where was Teri? When I was too nauseated to talk, she kept running in every minute to ask was I all right, and if I closed my eyes for a second she acted like I'd died. Why wasn't she here now when I needed company?

After I'd been waiting about ten years, Dr. Lucas showed up. Instead of examining me, he pulled up a chair and said, "I'd like to talk to you about your accident."

I didn't want to talk to him about my accident or anything else, but I'd been in the hospital long enough to know how things worked. The only way out of the prison of my bed was playing along. So, pretending I was Teri, the model of good behavior and respect for authority, I said, "It's all in the hospital records, but I guess you didn't have a chance to read them. I was redoing my room—I like to make things over—and I bought a mobile to hang from the ceiling. The super promised to put it up for me, but of course he never did. I fell trying to hang it myself. My surgeon says the problem with the leg comes from injuring the sciatic nerve when I hit the corner of my desk on the way down." That should show him I'd been paying attention.

When he just nodded, I gave him a Teri-type I'm-trying-to-please-you smile. "I guess I should've been more careful."

He nodded again—and waited. What was he waiting for? I couldn't think of anything else to say. I don't know how Teri does it.

I thought his face would crack when he finally opened his mouth to ask, "Have you had other accidents besides the mobile and the wheelchair?"

"Actually, my grandmother tells me that when I was six months old my mother brought me to visit and caught her heel on the top step. I flew out of her arms and tumbled down the whole flight of stairs. When she picked me up I was laughing."

The man had no sense of humor. He asked deadpan, "Any more recent accidents?" As if I made a habit of being run over by cars and having buildings collapse on me.

"No."

"Are you looking forward to going home?"

No, I liked being in a cage in the zoo. "Of course I am."

"Sometimes people are afraid of leaving a place where they feel safe and are taken care of. Your wheelchair accident did postpone your dismissal from the hospital."

"Are you accusing me of deliberately tipping over my chair to stay in the hospital? I never heard such a load of sh—such nonsense."

He went into a song and dance about not accusing me of anything but simply trying to guard against the possibility of any further accidents and if I would like to talk to him about my feelings he was available.

It dawned on me what kind of doctor he was. I almost told him I'd sooner have the *Enquirer* headline my feelings next to a story about a baby born with two heads. But there was probably a hospital rule about a psychiatrist saying you're sane before they let you out. I declared, "You don't have to worry. I'll be careful from now on."

Dr. Lucas left, but the idea he put into my head stayed. I'd already had two accidents. Suddenly I was terrified of a third. What if I fell again and paralyzed my other leg? What if I smashed my spine and couldn't move anything at all?

28

When the nurse came with my wheelchair, saying Dr. Lucas had given permission, I told her I was too tired to get up. I lay in bed (nothing could happen to me while I was lying still) until Teri came in.

She started telling me about working in the nursery this morning and being surprised at how darling newborn babies were.

I said, "The ridiculous psychiatrist who was just here would probably say that proves you really hate babies."

"I don't hate . . . What psychiatrist?"

I told her about Dr. Lucas and his idiotic accusation that I tipped over my wheelchair because I was afraid to go home. I started out making fun of him and ended up angry. I didn't mention his scaring me about another accident.

Teri made sympathetic noises until I got it off my chest. Then she said, "A doctor shouldn't upset you. He should understand what you're going through. But you *were* telling me it bothered you that your mother can't stay home to take care of you, that you'll have to have some stranger . . ."

If anyone else gave me that garbage, I'd open her head. But Teri honestly believes that doctors, nurses, priests, ministers, rabbis, parents, teachers, government officials, newspeople, and (for all I know) garbagemen are all wiser than we are. It was up to me to educate her. "You don't see that Dr. Lucas is a horse's tush because you can't believe that anyone in authority can ever be wrong. You always worry what the nurses will say or what's in the rule book. You're even intimidated by that old hag with the blue hair and lampshade earrings."

Teri's way of handling an argument she can't refute is

to switch the subject. She brushed back her hair so I could get a full view of her ears. "Henrietta says I shouldn't wear my grandmother's earrings to work. What do you think?"

I let her get away with it. "I think they're gorgeous." They were carved coral roses set in gold, the kind of antique jewelry you see featured in store windows on Madison Avenue.

"Rosanne's are nicer. She got the ones with the diamond chips because she's older."

To hear Teri tell it, Rosanne isn't only older; she is prettier, smarter, and braver. Rosanne really has Teri bamboozled. I said pointedly, "Liz Taylor has an umpteen-carat diamond ring. What does that have to do with *your* earrings being beautiful?"

I knew she got the point because she changed the subject again. "You don't ever wear earrings, do you?"

"My ears aren't pierced. When I considered having them done, my father said making holes in yourself is barbaric."

"If your father won't let you . . ."

That girl was incapable of finishing a sentence. She was also incapable of understanding that nobody told me what I could or couldn't do. If I did something to please somebody, that was my choice. Actually, since the divorce I'd crossed Dad off the list of people I wanted to please. *He* certainly hadn't pleased *me* by dumping Amanda for a jealous twit with big boobs and a vacuum between her ears. "I just decided. I'll have my ears pierced when I get out of this zoo."

"I could do them for you. I did a couple of girls in my old neighborhood."

Teri had unsuspected talent. "Okay. Do them now."

"Now? Here in the hospital? It's like a medical thing and I'm not supposed to . . ."

I gave her my fiercest stare and kept my eyes fixed on her until she said, "I need ice."

I pointed to the pitcher of ice water on my table.

"And a needle and thread."

I handed her the embroidery kit somebody in Amanda's office sent me. Who'd have thought I'd find a use for it?

"And earrings to put right in."

I fished out a ten-dollar bill. "See if they have some in the gift shop."

She shook her head. "They have to be gold. You can wear costume jewelry later, but your first earrings have to have gold posts."

That wrecked that. The way the accident had wrecked everything else in my life. Suddenly I was completely out of ideas. I gave up. I slid down under the sheet, pulled it up over my head, and closed my eyes. I closed out all the things I couldn't do, all the things I'd never do again.

Teri tugged at the sheet. "Sit up. I can't pierce your ears if you cover them."

I closed my eyes tighter and hung on. I wanted to hide under the sheet forever. I didn't want to see anything, feel anything, know anything.

She pried the material out of my grasp. "Maybe it's better if you lie down. In case you get dizzy or something. Rosanne did one of her friend's ears and the friend fainted dead away. Lucky Rosanne knew what to do."

What did she think I was? I sat up. "I don't faint."

She held an ice cube to my earlobe. "Don't look."

How can you look at your own ear? But I felt it. Ouch!

31

She iced the other ear. Actually, the whole thing didn't take very long, but I was glad when she was finished. Then it occurred to me. "You said I needed gold earrings."

She smiled and propped up the mirror on my table. I was wearing her coral and gold roses! They changed my whole face. They made me look beautiful. I didn't know what to say. I promised, "I'll give them back as soon as Amanda can buy me my own earrings. In a day or two."

"You have to keep these in for three or four weeks."

"But they were your grandmother's." If Gran were dead and I had something precious of hers, I'd never let it out of my hands.

"I trust you to take care of them."

My eyes got blurry. Wouldn't you know the bloody allergy would act up just when the first nice thing in ages happened to me? Swallowing the lump in my throat, I promised, "I'll take good care of them."

A nurse called Teri to wheel a patient to P.T. Teri called back that she was coming and told me hurriedly, "You have to turn the earrings twice a day and wash your earlobes with alcohol or peroxide. Peroxide doesn't sting as much. I'll bring you some tomorrow."

5

Teri

I never brought Valerie the peroxide. When I got home at five o'clock, Mama was lying down. She said it was nothing. "Just a little spotting, but the doctor said I should stay off my feet until it stops. He didn't say who should get your Papa's supper when he comes home starving. Doctors don't think about such things."

If Mama called the doctor it wasn't nothing, but I didn't want to worry her by showing I was worried. "Don't worry. I'll make supper."

"The spaghetti sauce is simmering on the stove and there's chop meat in the refrigerator." She gave me instructions like I'd never cooked before. She told me to be sure to skim the fat off the sauce, to use fresh garlic in the meatballs, and a dozen other things she knew I knew.

After all that, she didn't eat anything. When I brought her a plate of spaghetti on a tray, she said she wasn't hungry. I coaxed her to try, saying "*Mangia, mangia*, eat, eat" to make her smile. She didn't smile. She winced when

33

she sat up. I asked anxiously, "Are you having pains?"

"I'll be fine." But she didn't answer about the pains.

It was a long, draggy evening. Papa and I hardly said a word at supper. Neither of us wanted to say we were worried about Mama. I almost asked if he was going to call Rosanne and tell her Mama was sick. Only I didn't want to make a big thing out of what Mama said was nothing.

Her face looked so pasty when I took her untouched plate away that I almost said maybe we should call the doctor again, but something stopped me. I guess I figured if I didn't say anything, it would go away. So I washed and dried the dishes and straightened out the closet when I put them away. It was eight o'clock and still light out when I finished, even though it seemed more like four in the morning.

Mama was resting and Papa was reading the paper, but I couldn't sit still. Telling Papa I'd be back soon, I ran down to the drugstore for Valerie's peroxide.

I bought the peroxide and a Hershey bar, which I nibbled while I browsed the magazine rack to kill time. Leafing through *Popular Science*, a great idea for a project for next fall's science competition hit me. The science competition is a big thing in our school because Sister Josephine taught science before she became assistant principal. The girls write reports while the boys build things—although no report ever goes on to the citywide contest to compete for college scholarships.

Why shouldn't I build something? Not for a shot at a scholarship. Even though Valerie assumes that everyone goes to college, I probably won't. I don't want to be a nurse or a teacher. Anyway, I have ages to decide about college. The point is that I'd enjoy building a solar collector. I'm good with my hands, and there's no rule that girls have to write reports. Why shouldn't I do what I like and what I'm good at?

I read most of the magazine before I bought it, by which time it was dark out and Papa was probably thinking I'd been mugged. I hurried home.

As soon as I opened the apartment door, I knew something was terribly wrong. Papa was insisting to the phone, "No. No. You don't have to. All right. Meet us there."

He hung up and saw me. "Where were you? Mama started bleeding. I called the doctor and his service said to take her right to the emergency room. You stay with her while I go borrow Mrs. Nicolosi's old wheelchair and pull the car around."

I ran into the bedroom where Mama was lying on Papa's side of the bed looking pale as death. The towel spread across her side of the bed didn't cover all the bloodstains. I couldn't help myself. I burst out crying.

Mama shushed me. "It's nothing. Doctors make a big fuss so they can charge an arm and a leg."

I choked back my sobs. "It's silly of me to get upset. I know you'll be fine."

Papa came back with the wheelchair and helped Mama into it. I tucked the couch throw around her legs. Then I held the doors while he wheeled her into the elevator and then up the basement carriage ramp, the same route Mama'd planned for Valerie's visit.

I waited on the sidewalk while he settled her into the backseat of the car. Before I could get in next to her, Papa told me, "Take Mrs. Nicolosi back her wheelchair and be sure to double lock the apartment door behind you."

"But . . . but I'm coming with you."

"Aunt Paula's meeting us at the emergency room. You'll only be in the way. I'll call you after we see the doctor."

If Rosanne were here, he'd be begging her to stay by Mama's side every minute. Couldn't he see that I was as responsible as Rosanne? I was so hurt that I could hardly get the words out. "I won't be in the way. I'll be more help than Aunt Paula, who just bosses everyone around."

"Teresa, I can't argue with you now. Paula is Mama's sister."

And I'm her daughter. But I couldn't say it. I just stood there.

Papa slid behind the wheel and slammed the door. I watched him drive away. Then I went to return the wheelchair. Before I knew Valerie, I never seemed to see people in wheelchairs or on crutches. Now they were everywhere.

Mrs. Nicolosi insisted I stay for milk and cookies. Mrs. Nicolosi can chew your ear off. Listening to her was the last thing in the world I wanted to do, but I couldn't be rude. I sipped the milk and ate half a cookie while she went on and on about hoping that Mama wouldn't lose the baby. She counted on her fingers and decided that the baby might live if it was born now, but she wasn't sure that would be a blessing because her niece gave birth in her seventh month and the baby had four operations before it was a year old and was still sickly, and she wouldn't wish that on Mama because it was hard enough to have a baby at her age even if it was healthy.

However miserable I was when she started, I felt twice as bad when I finally got away. I locked the apartment

36

door like Papa told me and ran into my room and threw myself down on my bed and cried and cried. Until Mrs. Nicolosi brought it up, it hadn't occurred to me that Mama could lose the baby—or worse.

Crying didn't wipe the horrible thoughts out of my head. It just made my head hurt. I searched desperately through the bookcase I shared with Rosanne. It was mostly her nursing books with my *Popular Mechanics* stuffed in between. Finally, I found what I was looking for: the book of saints Aunt Paula gave me for my last birthday.

I went through the book saint by saint. Then I prayed to Saint Gerard Majella, patron of mothers and childbirth; Saint John of God, patron of the sick; and for good measure, Saint Rock, patron of invalids.

I prayed, "Please don't let anything happen to Mama. Keep her safe. And keep the baby safe. I'll never be ashamed of Mama's belly again if only you don't let anything happen."

It was three long, terrible hours before my prayers were answered. Worn out by worry, I fell asleep fully dressed on my bed. The ringing phone jolted me awake. I sprinted into the kitchen to answer it. When I picked up the phone, I was shaking so hard that I almost dropped it again.

Papa's voice said, "They stopped the bleeding. They're keeping Mama in the hospital overnight to make sure, and she has to stay in bed for a while when she comes home. But everything is going to be fine."

"And the baby?" I whispered.

"What? I can't hear you."

"The baby. Did Mama lose the baby?"

"Teresa, didn't you hear me? I said everything is fine."

*   *   *

The next morning, I called Mrs. McKay and told her I couldn't volunteer for a while because my mother was sick. She said she understood and added, "Your volunteer experience will make you a help to your mother."

I hadn't thought of it that way until Mrs. McKay said it, but I'd learned how to make patients comfortable in the hospital. By the time Papa brought Mama home that afternoon, I had everything ready for her: fresh sheets, extra pillows, a thermos of cold water on the night table, and a transistor radio and magazines in case she was feeling up to them.

Mama was so exhausted that she dropped off to sleep the minute she got into bed, and I didn't think she noticed what I'd done. But later, when Papa suggested asking Rosanne to come home, she said, "Let Rosanne be. Teresa and I will manage just fine."

And we did. My aunts brought cooked food and did the shopping and the laundry. But I was the one who took care of Mama. I changed her bed, helped her wash, and gave her lotion back rubs. It felt strange at first because Mama has always taken care of me. But when I overheard her telling Aunt Flo that I was better than a private nurse, I felt wonderful.

Aunt Flo said, "Teri is really growing up. I'll bet she can't wait to help you take care of the baby."

I wouldn't go so far as saying I was looking forward to it, but somehow I wasn't that upset about the baby anymore.

The summer was almost over before Mama was herself again. All that time I didn't hear a word from Valerie. At first I was too busy taking care of Mama to think about anyone else, but as Mama got better I kept expecting Valerie to call. Every time the phone rang, I ran for it. But it was always Rosanne or an aunt, uncle, cousin, or neighbor asking how Mama was.

Maybe Valerie didn't know my mother was sick. But Mrs. McKay must've told Henrietta, and telling Henrietta was like announcing it over the public address system. And Valerie had my phone number. I'd given it to her so she could call if she wanted me to bring her anything on my way to the hospital.

So why didn't she call now?

I didn't have to be as smart as Valerie to figure it out. Valerie was my friend when she was stuck in the hospital and needed me to get her juice or fix her bed when it jammed or run errands for her all over the place. She was my friend when I brought her cannoli and pierced her ears and lent her my earrings. But when she didn't need me anymore, she forgot I was alive.

What hurt most was that I'd started to believe that Valerie really liked me. How could I have been stupid enough to think that the know-it-all Ms. Valerie Ross would stoop to being my friend?

If it wasn't for my earrings, I'd have let Valerie grow a long white beard before I chased after her. But the earrings were valuable. She was the one who told me how valuable they were. I couldn't believe that even selfish brat Valerie would have the nerve to keep my grandmother's coral earrings.

She'd promised faithfully to return them as soon as she could take them out of her ears—which meant three or four weeks. I put a check on the kitchen calendar on the day she had my earrings three weeks. Then I gave her the benefit of the doubt, erased the check, and wrote it in again a week later. Today it was exactly four weeks and one day. Still no call, no insured special-delivery package, no nothing.

No way I was letting her get away with it. I pulled the phone book out of the closet and flipped to the *R*'s. There were a lot of Rosses, but only two on Central Park West: Leon Ross and A. Ross. *A* for Amanda. I dialed that number.

The phone ran six times. My heart was pounding louder than the ringing. Finally the phone was picked up. There was silence. Then she said, "Hello."

Just the one word, but I'd recognize that snobby voice from a single syllable. "Valerie," I said, "this is Teri."

"You took your own sweet time calling."

6

Valerie

⎯⎯

*B*eing in the hospital was so strange and horrible that I never quite believed it was real. I acted like the world's worst patient, complaining about the awful food and the effing lack of privacy, fighting with everyone who came near me. But even while I was making the worst scenes, I had a sense of play acting, of throwing myself headlong into the role of Valerie the Holy Terror. The whole time, there was a part of me that refused to believe that any of it—the hospital, the pain, the paralysis—was actually happening. Deep inside where nothing could reach it, I nursed a secret feeling that sooner or later the show would end and the curtain would come down and I'd be the way I was before the accident. That feeling kept me from giving up.

But when I got home, everything was ordinary and familiar. Everything was exactly as I left it to go to the hospital for the operation that had a 90 percent chance of making me walk again. Everything was just the way it was before I fell off the step stool. Everything was the same—except me.

I couldn't climb steps anymore. I couldn't walk across the room to get a book or play a tape. Sitting in my new wheelchair in my old, familiar room, I knew it was no play, no dream, no nightmare. It was real, horribly real. And it was forever.

When I came home, the energy drained out of my body like water out of the bathtub when you pull the plug. I went down the drain. What was left of me was too weak and tired to do anything. I'd been fitted for a leg brace and crutches in the hospital. They stood propped against the wall in my room while I slumped in the wheelchair, unable to even think of learning to use them.

Amanda was constantly on the phone making arrangements: finding someone to take care of me, getting me into a rehab center, arranging for home instruction in the fall. When she hung up, she'd tell me about each call as if it had something to do with me. I was too tired to listen.

She arranged for Mrs. Goldblatt, a retired nurse who lives down the hall, to look after me during the day. I called her Mrs. Go, which she thought was short for Goldblatt. Actually, it's short for "Go away and leave me alone."

Mrs. Go made me wash and dress and at least pick at my meals, but she accepted my excuses that it was too hot to go out, that I was too tired to exercise the leg, that I didn't know how to play gin rummy. The last was a lie. Dad's a gin rummy shark and he taught me all his strategies. Amanda must have told Mrs. Go that. Otherwise she wouldn't keep asking if I'd like a little game of gin and grinning like the Cheshire cat when I refused.

I knew Amanda had cautioned her not to push me. I'd heard them whispering about my needing time and space to get back to myself. As if I'd ever be myself again. As if I'd ever be anything but an exhausted cripple in a wheelchair.

Amanda didn't push me either—for a while. Then one evening (I don't know how long after I came home; why bother counting identical miserable days?) she suddenly announced that tomorrow I was starting at the center.

"Center? What center?"

"Valerie, I understand your being nervous about going, but please don't play games."

"I'm not playing a game. What do you expect me to say when you suddenly spring on me that you're shipping me off to some place I never heard of?"

"How can you say you never heard of the Center for Rehabilitative Medicine? I've been telling you all week about my struggle to get you in. They're the best in the country. If anyone can teach you to walk again, they can."

"No! I won't let you put me back in a hospital! They'll lock me up in a tiny cell again, and I'll go out of my mind."

"No one is locking you up. You know perfectly well that you are going as an outpatient three afternoons a week." Then she tried a different tack. "Val, please give the center a chance. I've arranged for an ambulette to take you and for Mrs. Goldblatt to go along. But if it will make you feel better, I'll take tomorrow afternoon off to go with you myself."

43

There was no point trying to explain that this was really the first I'd heard about the place. I believed that she told me all about it; she'd never believe that it hadn't registered. "You go to work."

"Are you sure?"

"I don't need you to come. And I definitely don't need Mrs. Go."

Amanda urged me to reconsider. I was firm. So the next afternoon Mrs. Go took me down to the street, watched the driver wheel me up the ramp into the ambulette, and went home.

When I saw what was in the ambulette, I was sorry I'd been a big shot. I'd assumed that an ambulette was like a cab—private. This was more like a subway car. There were already three other wheelchairs inside. For all I knew, we'd pick up cripples until we were packed in like the IRT in rush hour.

"Hello. I'm Derek. This is Fran and that's Lulu."

Derek spoke with a British public school accent and looked like Prince Charles. He was about twenty. I wondered if he'd gone to Oxford or Cambridge. Last summer in England, Gran introduced me to a neighbor's son home from Oxford for "the hols" and I really went for him. But no girl would go for Derek. Both his legs were in braces and he was braced halfway up his chest as well. I said, "I'm Valerie," and looked away.

Actually, there was no other place to look. Certainly not at either of the girls. Fran was about my age; she had a hook for a hand. Lulu was younger, and she didn't seem in bad shape until she tried to say "hi." Then her whole body shook with the effort and the word came out in a shower of spit. It was disgusting.

44

Derek asked if it was my first time at the center. When I grunted "yes," they immediately started telling me all about it. I stared at the floor, hoping if I didn't encourage them they'd leave me alone. Then I had to laugh at myself. If you like black humor, it was funny: *me* rejecting them because *they* were crippled.

So I put on my best charmed-to-meet-you face and tried to smile when they told funny stories (at least they thought the stories were funny; I found them gruesome) about the center. Lulu was the worst. I couldn't follow a word she said. I tried not to let her see me wiping away the drops of spit she sprayed on me. The next time I write a horror story, I'll set it inside an ambulette that never arrives at its destination.

We did get to the center eventually, and the ambulette driver unloaded our chairs like a furniture delivery. While I waited on the sidewalk, the others wheeled themselves through the self-opening door into the building. They waved good-bye. I waved back. After being so anxious to get rid of them, I felt strangely abandoned when the door closed behind them.

The driver delivered me to a woman at a desk who consulted a clipboard and called an orderly. The orderly pushed me down the hall, took me up in an elevator, and turned me over to a physical therapist who introduced himself as Rob. Rob was young, and his white T-shirt showed off strongly muscled arms. At another time in another place, I'd have enjoyed the view. Now I hardly spared him a glance as he wheeled me into a curtained-off booth and lifted me onto the padded table. I lay there stiff as chicken fresh out of the freezer.

Rob poked his finger into my calf muscles and asked

45

what I felt. When I said he was poking me, he told me to close my eyes and then tell him what I felt.

He poked, patted, and questioned up and down my leg. Sometimes I felt what he was doing and sometimes I didn't. Sometimes I wasn't sure. He kept it up so long that I demanded, "What bloody difference does it make what I feel if I can't move the leg?"

He said calmly, "Try to bend your knee."

Nothing happened. The leg lay there like a piece of a broken puppet.

He lifted the knee, lowered it gently, and lifted it again. "Try to work with me."

I didn't try because I didn't know how to try. If I wanted to bend my other knee, I wouldn't *try*. I'd just *bend* it. I couldn't bend the bad knee any more than I could see out of the back of my head. How do you *try* to see out of the back of your head?

Furious at Rob for demanding the impossible, I twisted my hip to yank the dead leg out of his hands. My thigh muscles went into severe cramp. I screamed in pain.

He massaged the cramp. "That's enough leg work for today. I'll get some wrist weights to strengthen your arms."

Back when I was a whole person, I played tennis with a wicked forehand, but my arms had softened to jelly in the hospital. When I complained that the weights were too heavy, Rob told me to try. I was getting to hate that word.

At the end of our half-hour session, Rob said I was scheduled for an hour of group occupational therapy to learn to dress myself, use an elevator, et cetera. The group turned out to be Derek, Fran, Lulu, and me.

Eunice, the occupational therapist, was one of those nauseating social-worker types who says *we*. "*We* want to learn to do things for *our*selves." "*We* want to be independent, don't *we*?" She made *me* want to sick up.

Since Eunice seemed to like being with pathetic cripples, I acted like one. When she made me practice taking stuff off a shelf with a long-handled gadget, I dropped everything. She took the gadget out of my hand and patiently showed me the proper way to use it. When she handed it back, I dropped the gadget. Although I should've gotten some satisfaction from the game, I didn't.

When O.T. was finally over, Derek, Fran, and Lulu wheeled themselves out of the room. I joined the cripples' parade.

By the time the ambulette arrived and the driver loaded us back in for the trip home, all I could think of was: I can't go through this three times a week. It didn't make things any better to have Derek tell me, "Eunice could help you if you'd let her."

"If I was on fire and Eunice had the only fire extinguisher in town, I wouldn't let her help me." Then I turned away from him and stared at the inside door handle for the rest of the ride.

Mrs. Go was waiting on the sidewalk for the ambulette. She took one look at me and said, "You need a drink."

For a second I thought she'd developed a sense of humor while I was gone, but she meant juice. She brought me a tall glass when we got into the apartment. Then she helped me out of my sweaty clothes and onto my shower bench. When I was clean, dry, and settled into bed, she asked, "Comfy?"

47

"I'm not too un-com-fort-a-ble."

"Then I'll go. If you need anything before your mother comes home, call me." She pushed the phone closer. "Remember, two rings and hang up." She reminds me every time. I didn't answer. She left.

When my phone rang a while later, I thought it was Mrs. Go checking on me. I let it ring. She didn't give up. I picked up the phone and counted to ten before I said, "Hello."

"Valerie, this is Teri."

Teri. It was a thousand years since I'd heard from her. Or given her a thought. Actually, I thought about her a lot while I was still in the hospital. When the blue-haired hag told me Teri'd stopped volunteering because her mother was sick, I almost called her. Then I thought, what if her mother is seriously ill? What if her mother is dying? (Those are the thoughts you have in the hospital.) And I couldn't bring myself to pick up the phone. Anyway, it was really up to Teri to call me. She was the one who disappeared without a word.

When she didn't call, I figured her enthusiasm for playing Mother Teresa to a cripple had worn off. Or maybe she'd simply found more interesting things to do. In either case, I put her out of my mind—along with tennis, going to the movies, and cutting my own toenails.

Hearing her voice again, I realized I'd missed her. But I played it cool. "You took your own sweet time calling."

There was a little gasp. How easy it was to get a rise out of her. I started to enjoy myself for the first time all day. All week. All summer.

Teri said, "I'm calling because I want my grandmother's earrings back."

48

Automatically, I touched my ears. The earrings were still exactly where Teri had put them. I was supposed to turn them or something, but I'd forgotten. I'd had more important things to think about—or rather, to keep from thinking about.

I said, "Come get them."

7

Teri

———

*V*alerie said "come get them" like she was lending me *her* earrings. I almost said she was awfully high and mighty for an earring thief. Then I remembered that she couldn't very well run over or hop on a bus to drop them off. Right away, I felt guilty.

Okay. Maybe she didn't mean to keep my earrings, and sure, it was up to me to pick them up because she couldn't walk. But there was nothing wrong with her hands. She could dial a phone as easily as me, but she sat and waited for me to call and then expected me to come running when she crooked her little finger. Well, I wasn't in a hurry. I said, "It's too late tonight and tomorrow I've got the dentist and Sunday the family . . ."

"Monday, Wednesday, and Friday I'm at the center."

"The next weekend Rosanne's coming home from the country."

"Isn't that Labor Day weekend? I'm surprised they

50

don't need the waitresses to work through Labor Day."

She caught me. Valerie's better at playing games than I am. "I meant she's coming home the Tuesday after Labor Day."

"Then make it the following Thursday. Actually, you might as well come for lunch. Mrs. Go likes to cook. Ta." And she hung up.

Mrs. Go gave us noodle soup, chicken salad sandwiches, and chocolate cake for lunch. It was all homemade, and I told her she was a good cook. She said she was a good gin-rummy player too. She told me how she finally convinced Valerie to learn, only to discover that Valerie was a card shark. I said I didn't have much card sense. Mrs. Go said cards weren't important. Valerie didn't say anything. She didn't say two words the whole meal. Why did she invite me to lunch if she was going to sit mashing her cake to crumbs like I wasn't there?

Since I was there, Mrs. Go went back to her own apartment. I told Valerie, "She's a nice lady."

Valerie looked at me like I just said little green men were climbing out of flying saucers in the living room. "You are unreal." Then she turned to stare out the window. I couldn't see what she was looking at.

I cleared my throat. "About my earrings . . ." She was still wearing them.

"I can't work the catches."

"Squeeze and then pull." I bent over her to do it. "Your ears don't look completely healed. Are you cleaning them with peroxide every day?"

"I forgot."

"You'll get infections. How could you forget?"

"I was too busy touring Europe in my Rolls-Royce and skiing in the Alps."

She was right about my being unreal. How could I keep forgetting there was anything wrong with her? Here she was sitting in a wheelchair right in front of me, but I didn't remember she was disabled till she rubbed my nose in it. I felt so stupid.

I made a big deal out of cleaning her ears with alcohol and slathering them with Bacitracin ointment. She let me fuss over her like it didn't have anything to do with her. Like she didn't care if her ears fell off.

It made me nervous for her to be so . . . so out of it. But I acted like nothing was wrong. I told her the holes would close up unless she kept wearing earrings so I'd put in a pair of hers. When she didn't answer, I asked loudly, "Do the earrings your mother bought you have gold posts? Where are they? I'll get them."

"No."

"No, they don't have gold posts or no, don't get them?"

She answered impatiently, like I was the one not paying attention, "I told you I forgot all about the bloody earrings. I don't have any. If you want yours, take them. I couldn't care less if the effing holes close up."

I was so glad to have her acting like herself again that I said, "Don't be silly. Keep these till you get your own. I'll put them back in."

She relented, "When my father calls to ask what I want for my birthday, I'll say earrings. There's nothing else I want anyway. Except a new leg. You don't happen to know where he could buy me a new leg, do you?"

"I wish I did."

"It was a rhetorical question, but thanks anyway."

I said, "My birthday's this month too. What day is yours?"

"September seventeenth."

"Mine's the thirtieth. I'll be fifteen. How about you?"

"Fifteen."

"We're practically twins." I was surprised. I thought she was a lot older than me because she's so sophisticated. "Rosanne is making me a little party. What are you doing?"

"Having brunch on a yacht."

I really asked to feel her out about coming to my party, but trust Valerie to knock my socks off. Brunch on a yacht! I never ate brunch anywhere. At home we have breakfast, lunch, and supper. Not brunch. And certainly not on a yacht. "Did you ever go before? What's it like?"

She told me her parents always took her to Sunday brunch in a restaurant for her birthday. When her father stopped going after the divorce, her mother kept up the tradition. This year they were going on a World Yacht cruise. It seems there's this real yacht fixed up inside like a restaurant and you eat at a table looking out at the water while the boat cruises all the way around Manhattan. I never heard of anything so fancy.

I was completely bowled over when Valerie said casually, like she was offering me another piece of cake, "Amanda says I can ask a friend. Want to come?"

"Oh, yes!" I was so excited I almost hugged her, but you have to play it cool with Valerie. "I mean, okay. When?"

"The Sunday after my birthday. There's a calendar in that drawer. Look up the date."

The brunch turned out to be the same weekend as my

party, which Rosanne was making early because the baby is due soon. I asked, copying Valerie's it's-all-the-same-to-me manner, "Why don't you come to my party too? It'll be like a two-day birthday celebration."

"A Chinese birthday? Interesting. Are you planning a couples party or inviting girls and guys separately?"

I had no idea what a Chinese birthday was, but that wasn't the problem. The problem was telling Valerie it was only going to be girls from the old neighborhood. Of course, we hadn't invited anyone yet and Rosanne is always after me to stop being so shy and I'm the most shy with boys so . . . "I think separate works better." Though where I was going to find boys to invite separately, I didn't know.

Luckily, some of Valerie's smarts seemed to have rubbed off on me. I suggested, like it wasn't important one way or the other, "We could make it a double birthday party. You know, like a double wedding. You ask half the guests. Since you probably know more boys than I do, it's okay if you ask a couple of extra boys."

"We'd need a party theme. Autumn leaves? Too trite. Literary characters? Too arty. I know, come as your favorite person. No, as the person you'd most like to be."

"You mean a costume party?"

"Costumes are so ordinary. We'll have people carry some symbol of their identity."

Symbols sounded more complicated than costumes, but I didn't get a chance to say so. She rushed on, "For decorations we'll have posters of famous people. Make a list. Beethoven, Virginia Woolf, Madonna, Darryl Strawberry, Mother Teresa." She grinned at me. "Definitely Mother Teresa. And more famous people on the invitations. Now

54

what kind of music? Let's look through my tapes." She spun her chair around and wheeled full speed ahead to her room.

Then back to the living room to consult the encyclopedia. Earlier, I was worried because Valerie seemed so out of it. Now I couldn't keep up with her. Ideas spouted out of her as fast and furious as corn popping on the stove. I made so many lists that I needed a list of the lists.

We were still at it when the apartment door opened and a woman came in carrying a flat cardboard box. She had to be Valerie's mother, but she didn't look like a mother. She looked like she belonged on "L. A. Law." I could see why Valerie called her by her first name.

She said, "Dinner's early because I have a meeting tonight. I brought a mushroom pizza." Then she saw me and smiled. "Hello. You must be Teri. Valerie mentioned you were coming. For your earrings, wasn't it?"

I nodded. I can never think of what to say when I meet new people.

Valerie told her mother, "I invited Teri on the yacht cruise."

"How nice." She smiled at me again.

I smiled back. I still couldn't think of anything to say. Then I realized she was waiting for me to leave so they could eat. Mama would've invited me to stay even if it was just pizza. Mama would've made a salad and . . . But Mama never had a meeting after supper. I said quickly, "I have to go now. See you at the yacht."

"I'm ordering a limousine for Valerie. You're welcome to come here and ride with us."

A limousine to take me to a yacht! Wait till the girls at school heard about this. "Thank you, Mrs. Ross."

"Ms. Scott."

When I looked puzzled, she explained, "I've always kept my maiden name. As things turned out, it was a good decision, wasn't it?"

Now I really didn't know what to say. Somehow I didn't expect her to make a joke—especially not that kind of joke. So I said I had to run, and ran.

I was so excited about having a double birthday party with a theme and symbols and everything and then the very next day going on a yacht cruise with Valerie and her mother that I ran halfway home before it dawned on me that with all the lists Valerie and I made, we'd skipped the most important one. We never made a guest list. I slowed down to a walk and started worrying about who to ask to such a fabulous party. Nobody I knew seemed good enough.

8

Valerie

I must've been stark, raving bonkers. Why else would I get involved in Teri's idiotic birthday party? Like a double wedding, the girl said. She was pathetic. And I was crazy.

Once a night's sleep had restored me to my right mind, I saw that the only reasonable course of action was to tell her that the deal was off. Temporary insanity is a defense in court. It would have to do for Teri.

I stared at the phone. I even picked it up. I couldn't do it. I couldn't disappoint Teri. It would be like grabbing a lollypop out of a baby's mouth.

I yelled for Mrs. Go. When she meandered in, wiping her hands on her apron, I demanded to know if she'd forgotten that the ambulette was coming any minute. Usually she reminds me and I take my sweet time getting ready. I added, "Oh, I think I'll take my brace and crutches today. Please get them."

I had plenty of time to regret rushing. I was downstairs

twenty minutes before the ambulette was due. The seconds crawled by like an endless parade of ants while I sat on the sidewalk in my wheelchair awkwardly clutching the brace and crutches laid across the armrests—an object of pity for the whole neighborhood. I glared at the passersby so fiercely that they looked hastily away. But I knew that all the glaring in the world couldn't stop them feeling sorry for me.

When I finally escaped into the ambulette (naturally, it was late), Derek said, "I see you brought your brace and crutches."

"No, these are band instruments. The driver is going to play while we all dance."

He screwed an imaginary monocle into his eye and peered through it. "May I have the first waltz?"

I forced a smile. I could really like Derek—if he weren't a cripple. Correct that. I could like him if he didn't *accept* being a cripple.

When I first met my ambulette mates, I thought that they were born disabled, that they'd had a lifetime to get used to being half human, that I was the only one struck down by lightning out of a clear, blue sky. Then I found out that Derek fell off the roof trying to rescue his cat, Fran was in a car accident, and even Lulu, who had a rare disease, only got so bad in the last year or so.

How did they bear it? Didn't they imagine turning time back to before the accident and doing it all over and coming out safe and whole? Didn't they wake at night believing they could declare, "I'm getting out of here," and fly away from their broken bodies like butterflies leaving their cocoons? Didn't they scream in their heads, "No! I won't be this way! I won't!"? Was I the only one?

58

Thinking about their acceptance of their horrible fate upset me so much that I didn't want to talk to them. I didn't even want to look at them. It was as if it would rub off on me if I got too close to them. So I sat fiddling with my brace for the rest of the ride, closing the Velcro fasteners and yanking them open again.

First one out of the ambulette, I wheeled myself to the visitors' elevator so I wouldn't have to ride up with the others. The patients' elevator has a man to run it and help you in and out. The visitors' elevator is automatic; you have to push the buttons yourself and get through the door before it closes on you. It was living dangerously to try it for the first time while balancing a brace and crutches.

Although I was sweating when I reached P.T., I made it.

Rob was waiting for me. I pointed the brace at him like a dueling sword. "I can't put this thing on by myself."

"It's easier lying down. I'll show you."

"Another time. Teach me to walk with it first. I have to be walking by the nineteenth."

One thing about Rob: he's unflappable. He didn't say a word about my finally bringing the brace after "forgetting" it all last week. He didn't even ask why the nineteenth. He just put the brace on for me and said, "That gives us today and three sessions next week. Let's start in the bars."

That meant no curtained-off booth. It meant working in the main gym, where everyone could enjoy watching me fall on my face. I couldn't do it. I couldn't make a bloody fool of myself with everyone staring at me. I wanted to crawl under my wheelchair and hide. I said, "What are we waiting for?"

The bars were at hand height, three feet apart. They

divide the end of the gym into lanes. Each lane was thirty feet long. It seemed more like thirty thousand as I stood at the head of the center lane with my hands curled tightly around the cold metal bars on either side of me. I stared down at my sneakers.

Rob said, "Look in the mirror."

The end wall of the gym was one huge mirror. I couldn't bear to look at the reflection of the poor cripple with the brace on her leg. That wasn't me. I wouldn't let it be me. I wanted to smash the effing mirror.

And crawl back into my wheelchair.

No! I'd never had a birthday party before and there was no way I was going in a wheelchair. I demanded of Rob, "What am I supposed to see in the mirror?"

"See where your weight is. See how heavily you're leaning on the bars. Shift your weight onto your left leg."

The left is my good leg. I did what he said.

"Swing your right leg forward from the hip."

I couldn't do it.

I did it.

"Now let your right leg take the weight while you bring the left forward. Don't worry. The brace will support you."

Don't worry. He might as well say "don't breathe." I held my breath as the bad leg took my weight. (Some of my weight, anyway; I was still leaning heavily on the bars.) I was sure the leg wouldn't hold. I was sure it would crumple like a soggy piece of cardboard.

Rob said, "Again."

Again? I looked in the mirror and saw with wonder that I was two steps down the lane. I'd walked two steps!

I walked the whole length of the lane. Rob helped me turn around, and I walked the whole way back. Then I did it again. I was really tired by the time he settled me back into my wheelchair, but it was different from the exhaustion I'd felt since I left the hospital. It was the way I used to feel after a fast set of tennis. Tired and good.

Eunice did her best to ruin my good feeling when I got to O.T. She had one of her cutesy ideas: We would have a "cozy little gathering." She appointed Fran hostess. The rest of us were guests. Fran had to serve while we practiced maneuvering our wheelchairs up to the table, passing food without dropping it in our laps, et cetera. To make it more "fun," Eunice provided real milk (warm) and real cookies (stale). I would have liked to add some real sick-up.

Fran made my day by knocking over the milk container first try. After that it was all downhill.

Eunice announced in her let's-not-be-discouraged-by-a-tiny-setback voice that there was enough milk left for a half glass apiece. So the charade went on. Couldn't Eunice see how idiotic it was to make us pretend we were normal people doing normal things? Couldn't she see how pathetic her cozy gathering was?

People see what they want to see. I began to wonder if I was as blind as Eunice. Were all my great ideas for our double birthday party as stupid as Eunice's? It was one thing to walk down the bars twice; getting around on crutches for an entire evening was a whole different ballgame. Actually, what was the effing big difference between crutches and a wheelchair? Why was I knocking myself out to learn to use the bloody brace? And who was I going to invite to the party?

61

9

Teri

———

Even though school was starting, all I could think about was our birthday weekend. I had long telephone conferences with Valerie, who kept coming up with exciting new ideas for our party. I ran over there to pick up the invitations she made on her computer and her sketches for the decorations. We made a good team; she was the brains and I was the feet. While she thought, I made props for the games and shopped for the food.

I'd been nervous about telling Rosanne what we were up to because she'd planned a get-together with the girls from the old neighborhood. But as Valerie says, not to worry. A theme party was right up Rosanne's alley. She had so many suggestions that I sometimes felt like a messenger between her and Valerie.

Though I did come up with one idea, one I didn't discuss with Rosanne or Valerie. Rosanne decided the living room would hold twelve to fifteen people, or six or seven guests each. Valerie asked four guys and two girls. I had five girls but only one boy—Peter, who's always explaining things to me at the science club meetings. Even though Peter is a senior and president of the science club, he's still only one guy. Then I had this idea. My cousin Marc is gorgeous enough for two guys, and he says I'm his favorite little cousin. I'd ask him as a favor to pick Valerie up and drive her over. Then I'd casually invite him to stay for the party.

The party was about to begin. If Valerie or Rosanne had any more ideas, it was too late. I put my birthday present to Valerie on the table. I bought her these wild earrings, big hanging clusters of what the saleswoman called faux jewels. I'd look like a freak in them, but they go with Valerie's personality.

I checked my beautiful new watch, a birthday present from Mama and Papa. Five to eight. The invitations were for eight o'clock, and I was getting more nervous by the second. I knew exactly how the bride feels when they play the wedding march. I worried that my new dress was too dressy. I fiddled with my Indian bangle bracelet, the symbol of the person I was supposed to most want to be. Maybe I should've borrowed Rosanne's gold cross for my symbol, or picked an inventor or somebody. I only chose Mother Teresa because Valerie expected me to.

The doorbell rang, and Rosanne told me to answer it. I hoped it was Julia or Patsy. Maybe I wouldn't be so nervous meeting Valerie's friends with someone I knew by my side. My luck, it was a strange boy. I went all tongue-tied.

More and more people arrived, but—after all our thought and work—the party didn't get off the ground.

My old friends clustered together on one side of the room and Valerie's friends stayed on the other.

Then Valerie made her entrance. It's funny how you think you know somebody, but you don't really. The Valerie who walked in was an elegant stranger. Yes, I said *walked*. With those metal crutches that fit onto your arms. She was wearing a slim, black velvet pantsuit that set off her blond hair and green eyes. With diamond studs sparkling in her ears, she was absolutely stunning. Even the crutches seemed like part of her outfit. And Marc was the perfect escort for her.

Three people jumped up and offered Valerie their chairs. She laughed. I don't think I ever heard her laugh before. It was a little chuckle that told you something clever was coming. "I choose the papa bear chair."

When she was settled, she held out her crutches. "Marco, please get rid of these for me." She pronounced his name in the Italian way, trilling the *r*. Marc didn't seem to mind. He sat down near Valerie. It was clear I wasn't going to have to convince him to stay for the party.

From the moment Valerie arrived, the party was a success. She ran it from Papa's chair like a director filming a movie. First she directed each of us to show our symbols so the others could guess who we most wanted to be. Julia, who's known me forever, guessed Mother Teresa as soon as it was my turn. Valerie stumped us with George Sand. I didn't know he—I mean, she—was a woman.

Then Valerie organized the games. Some of the games were very intellectual, some were silly, and some made you say things that aren't really dirty but sound that way if you have that sort of mind. It didn't really matter what the game was; Valerie made it fun.

Rosanne was supposed to be chaperoning us. Otherwise Mama and Papa would never have gone to Aunt Flo's for the evening. But even she got caught up in the fun.

We'd planned dancing after the games, so at Valerie's signal I put on the first tape. But we hadn't planned (at least I hadn't) for Valerie to announce, "The birthday girl will start off the dancing. Teri, pick a partner."

Although Rosanne had taught me to dance "just in case," I was positive I'd trip over my feet with everyone watching. But Valerie gave me no choice. I picked Peter for my partner.

Peter's so quiet—except when he's explaining science—that I was surprised by how well he danced. And how nice it felt to dance with him. Everyone clapped for us. For the first time in my life, I enjoyed being in center stage.

Of course, Valerie couldn't dance. So Marc didn't either. I noticed how close he stayed to Valerie all evening, like she had him on a leash. The way he smiled at her, you'd never guess he only brought her as a favor to me because I'm his favorite cousin.

Marc wasn't the only one. All the boys kept running over to Valerie's chair like ants heading for the sandwiches at a picnic. I can't figure out how she attracted them. There are these girls at school who throw themselves at the boys. They giggle and wiggle and practically wear signs saying, "notice me." Valerie wasn't like that at all. She didn't do anything special. She was just . . . Valerie.

Rosanne announced it was time to eat. Mama had made her special eggplant Parmesan and garlic bread; Rosanne and I did the spaghetti and salad. Julia came into the kitchen to help us serve. Her very first words were, "Your friend Valerie is so brave. And such fun."

Julia's my oldest friend even if we only see each other in school since I moved uptown. Did she say my party was great? Did she tell me how good I looked dancing with Peter? No, she said *Valerie* was terrific. It seems the boys weren't the only ones impressed with Valerie.

All right, so I was jealous. But only for a second. Then I realized Julia was complimenting me as well. I mean, if Valerie is special and I'm Valerie's chosen friend, that makes me special too, doesn't it?

So I told Julia how Valerie went from being flat on her back to a wheelchair to her first time on crutches tonight. Julia hung on my words so she could repeat them to the girls at school who weren't lucky enough to be invited to the party.

Rosanne asked, "Are you gossiping or serving?" and we ran to put the platters on the table. Everyone dived in.

When what was left of the food was cleared away, Valerie and I opened our presents. Rosanne gave me a bulky sweater she knitted for me in the country. Marc brought me a sterling silver necklace from Aunt Flo and Uncle Charley and a matching bracelet from him.

Valerie said the earrings I bought her were "wonderfully kooky" and she loved them. As I opened the blouse from Julia and the interlocking-gears puzzle from Peter, I kept expecting the next box to be from Valerie. It never was.

As I cleared away the crumpled wrapping paper, I kept smiling so nobody would see how hurt I was. Rosanne says I get hurt too easily. Knowing Rosanne was right didn't change the way I felt. I mean, Valerie and I never said anything about giving each other presents. But I ran all over town for the perfect present for her, and she didn't care enough to even give me a candy bar. I know she can't go shopping, but she could've asked her mother or Mrs. Go.

They say bad things come in threes. The first was not getting a present from Valerie. The second was Mama and Papa coming home. Mama stood talking to the girls from the old neighborhood about their families. She sent messages to their mothers and aunts and grandmothers. One of the boys rushed to give her his chair like he was scared she'd have the baby in the middle of the floor if she didn't sit down right away. She filled the whole chair and then some. I wanted to go through the floor.

Not so much because of the baby. While Mama had to stay in bed so she wouldn't bleed, she kept telling me how she was depending on my help when the baby came, and I got to thinking it might not be so bad—sort of like having a live doll. (Even though I always liked Lego better than dolls as a kid.) What was getting to me was the way Mama *looked*. Like a balloon about to burst.

If I was the goody-goody Valerie says I am, I wouldn't be ashamed of my mother looking so . . . so pregnant in front of Valerie and her friends. But I bet none of their mothers has a big belly. Valerie's mother's waist is smaller than mine.

The third bad thing was Papa taking his mandolin out of the closet. I couldn't meet Valerie's eyes. She'd never believe how hard I worked talking Rosanne into talking Mama and Papa into going out for the evening. Now they were turning our exciting theme party into a . . . Why couldn't they see that they didn't belong, that they were humiliating me in front of Valerie and her friends?

.

Papa played "Funiculi-Funicula." Mama sang along, and Rosanne and Marc joined in. Then they did "O Sole Mio." Even though I know all the words in Italian, I kept my mouth shut so nobody would think I was part of what they were doing.

It was worse for me than Valerie coming to Sunday dinner and seeing Aunt Paula in her black mourning dress and Uncle Charley chewing on his cigar. At least I could agree with her that the dress and cigar are terrible. But I love Papa's music. I'm proud he can play anything he hears even though he never had a lesson in his life. It's just that I didn't want him to play *now*. I didn't want everyone thinking we were a bunch of peasants from the old country.

Papa played a couple more old songs, and Valerie and her friends pretended to enjoy them. I knew they were just being polite. I knew they were feeling sorry for me because my parents wouldn't let me have a proper birthday party.

One of the boys asked Papa, "Do you know 'Graceland'?"

"Sing it."

He sang, and Papa picked up the melody. Most of the other kids sang along. I couldn't join in because I didn't know the words. When I didn't want to sing, I knew the words. When I wanted to, I didn't.

10

Valerie

—◆—

*I*was back in the effing wheelchair.

Amanda tried to comfort me. "Last night was your first time on crutches, and you did amazingly well. However, you can't expect to throw the wheelchair away immediately."

That's exactly what I expected. When I walked into the party last night, I felt as if I were on a rocket to the moon. But the rocket fizzled out on the launch pad this morning, leaving me with pain in my leg and a blister on my foot. I demanded, "If the bloody nerve is too damaged to make the leg move, how can it make it hurt?"

"The doctor says the pain is a good sign."

"If the effing leg fell off, he'd say it was a good sign."

"Valerie, I wish you wouldn't talk like that."

"All right. If the perfectly wonderful leg fell off."

She said in her cheer-Valerie-up voice, "The pain means the nerve isn't completely dead. It means there's hope

69

for the return of some movement in the leg. Hope for even more progress than you're already making."

If I was making such wonderful progress, why was I going to my birthday brunch in a wheelchair? And why did everyone always act so bloody optimistic? I hate it. I sat there (in my wheelchair) with a patient look on my face (to show I wasn't buying it) until Amanda finished telling me how well I was doing. Then I said, "Since I don't have to worry about walking in them, I think I'll wear heels. Spike heels."

Teri arrived while I was putting in the flashy earrings she'd given me. They hurt my ears, but I didn't care. Maybe the earrings would make people look at my face instead of my legs. I tossed back my hair. "How do they look?"

"Fine."

I ignored her down-in-the-mouth expression. I was in no mood for someone else's misery. "Here are your grand-mother's earrings back. Sorry to keep them so long."

"That's okay," making it clear that something was definitely not okay.

I ran out of patience. "What do *you* have to be so glum about? Cut it out or I'll keep your birthday present." I pushed the gift-wrapped package toward her.

"You bought me a birthday present?" Her face lit up like the Empire State Building at night.

"Actually, I didn't buy it. Open it and you'll see." Then the penny dropped; the long face was because she thought I wasn't giving her a present. Didn't she realize I couldn't carry it to the party with my arms in crutches? How selfish did she think I was?

She removed the paper, examined the leather-bound

book carefully, opened it to the title page, and read out, *Sonnets from the Portuguese.* Then she read the names and dates written under the title, " 'Emily Scott, 1939; Valerie Ross, 1992.' Scott? That's . . ."

"Gran. It was her book when she was my age. She gave it to me the last time I was in England. Since you lent me your grandmother's earrings . . ." My voice trailed off. Teri's habit of not finishing sentences seems to be catching.

"It's a beautiful present. Especially because it was your grandmother's. Knowing how you feel about her, how much you miss her, I can't believe you gave me this. It means we're truly friends, doesn't it?"

I'd given Teri Gran's book to make up for the times I took it out on her because I was feeling bloody-minded. It follows logically that if you're willing to part with something you value to make someone else feel good, you value that person. But there are some things you don't *say.* At least, *I* don't say them. So I just gave a little nod.

Amanda came in to tell us the limo was here.

The driver gave us the VIP treatment. He helped me into the limo as if he were handing the queen down from her throne. Then, with a little bow, he held the car door for Amanda and Teri. I got a kick out of how impressed Teri was. Her face shows everything she's thinking. She'd make a rotten gin rummy player. Mrs. Go would slaughter her.

During the drive, Amanda asked how we enjoyed the party last night. Teri waxed enthusiastic about the theme and the games. I returned the compliment by describing the songfest and the way Teri's father can play any song he hears.

71

Teri's face announced she was unhappy. Thinking she was feeling sorry for me because her father played music for her friends at her party and my father wasn't coming to my birthday celebration, I asked her, "Did you notice the earrings I wore last night? Dad sent them with a note saying, 'Diamonds are a girl's best friend.' "

"The earrings are beautiful, but I don't agree with the note. People are people's best friends." Her face showed that she was absolutely sincere.

I said of course she was right. Her naïveté amuses me and cheers me up. I was glad I'd invited her along.

When we arrived at the pier, a flunky in a glitzy uniform spotted me in my wheelchair and came running. Without asking my permission—or saying a word to me—he stepped behind my chair and starting pushing me toward the yacht's gangplank.

I yelled, "Whoa!"

The flunky stopped and looked vaguely around as if the command had come from outer space. Several people turned to see what was going on. Dropping my voice so they couldn't hear, I said, "You're intruding on my personal space. How would you like someone to suddenly pick you up and carry you?"

He didn't answer. Obviously the idea was too complicated for his small brain. So I said, "I can manage by myself," and wheeled rapidly away from him.

I crossed the pier, gathering up speed that should have taken me straight up the gangplank. It didn't. Strips of wood were nailed across the gangplank like steps. I guess they were supposed to keep people from slipping. They kept me from moving. I got stuck on them like a bug on a pin. My struggles to get free didn't help any more than

72

the bug's wriggling. The people who'd been watching looked away in embarrassment. I've never felt so humiliated in my life.

To make my humiliation complete, the flunky rescued me. I hung my head in shame as he pushed me onto the yacht and parked me at a table with a view of the river. Amanda and Teri followed and sat down on either side of me.

The view was perfect. The river sparkled blue-green and silver under a clear, sunny sky. If I turned my head, I could probably see the George Washington Bridge upriver and the Statue of Liberty downriver. I didn't turn my head. I stared down at the table.

The table was perfect too. Snowy tablecloth, elegant china and silver, and a fresh-fruit centerpiece.

I wasn't perfect. I was in a wheelchair with a paralyzed leg. I was sure everyone was wondering what such a damaged person was doing in such a perfect place.

When Amanda asked "Isn't this nice?" as if nothing had happened on the gangplank, I couldn't answer.

Teri answered enough for both of us. She went into a long spiel about how lovely the yacht was with an orchestra and everything, how she'd never been to such a fancy place, and could she take a kiwi fruit from the centerpiece home for her sister. I thought Teri was supposed to be so shy.

The orchestra broke into "We're Off to See the Wizard" and the yacht started downriver. Teri applauded, stopping in midclap when she realized nobody else was applauding.

Amanda suggested we sample the buffet. Teri leaped eagerly to her feet. I didn't budge. I wasn't hungry.

Amanda stood and waited for me. Teri begged, "Come

on, Valerie. Before all the best stuff is gone." Couldn't they see how awful I felt? I wheeled myself across the room to get away from them.

People at buffets always crowd around the table and fill their plates as if there's a prize for grabbing the most food the fastest. But when they saw my wheelchair, they pointedly stepped aside to make room for me. I recognized some of the people who'd watched my humiliation on the gangplank. I wanted to dig a hole, crawl into it, and pull the hole in after me. I held my head high and wheeled up to the buffet table.

Maybe the table was the right height to see the food if you were standing on two good legs. From down where I was sitting, I had a view of the edge of the tablecloth. I spun my chair around and sped away. If I'd been on dry land, I'd have headed straight home to lock myself in my room and never come out again even if it meant first wheeling myself fifty blocks through heavy traffic.

Teri came running after me. "You wait at the table while I go see what there is. Then I'll get you whatever you want."

I waited because I couldn't figure out a way to climb through the unopenable window and throw myself into the river.

She came back to report enthusiastically, "There are eggs and bacon and a fancy chicken dish and roast beef and something your mother says is seafood crêpes. And potatoes and salad and muffins and stuff. What should I get you?"

"I don't care." Whoever said misery likes company didn't know what he was talking about. What misery really wants is to be left alone. I knew I wasn't being fair to Teri.

She was only trying to be kind and considerate. But I was sick of people being kind to me. I was sick of needing people to be kind. I was sick of being a bloody cripple. The thought of being crippled for the rest of my life was too much to bear.

Teri went away. When she and Amanda returned, Teri was carrying two plates. She put one in front of me. "I got you a little of everything."

I managed a "thanks" and picked moodily at a seafood crêpe while we cruised to the Statue of Liberty and around the Battery. Teri ate like food was going out of style. Between mouthfuls, she exclaimed over every landmark like a tourist from Minnesota or Mongolia. She kept telling me to look.

I didn't look. I jabbed holes in my roast beef with my knife and watched the blood ooze out.

Amanda had the good sense to leave me alone. She asked Teri about her school and family. Teri finally caught on and stopped bothering me.

Here's some free advice for helpful people: When someone's miserable, don't try to cheer her up. Don't tell her to look at the UN building or the pretty sailboat. Understand that sometimes a person needs to be miserable, that sometimes misery is all she has to hold onto.

Left to my own devices, I wallowed in my misery for a while. I sneaked quick looks around to catch people staring at me. But they were all gobbling, gabbing, or staring at the view.

Eventually all the eating around me started to make me hungry. I nibbled a muffin. Then I tasted the chicken. They were good. Good enough to make me guilty about sitting like a ghost at the feast. Amanda had gone to a lot of trouble for my birthday, and Teri was all excited about coming. I made up my mind to be sociable if it killed me.

Teri was proudly telling Amanda about Rosanne training to be a nurse. Teri's constantly taking a backseat to her sister gets on my nerves. I asked, "Why is Rosanne becoming a nurse? Couldn't she get into medical school?"

Teri looked happy that I was joining in. "Rosanne didn't apply to medical school. It's much too expensive. Besides, she's a girl."

"I didn't think she was a giraffe."

"You know what I mean."

I sure did. I asked in the patient voice you use to teach a four-year-old her address in case she gets lost, "Remember the groups of interns doing the rounds in the hospital? Didn't you notice that some of them were female? Has it escaped your attention that more and more women are becoming doctors and lawyers and engineers?"

"Sure, a girl can be a doctor, but it means giving up everything else. Rosanne wants to get married and have babies. She wants to lead a normal life."

I was beginning to enjoy myself. Actually, there's nothing like a good argument to perk you up. "Are you saying that women who don't marry and have children aren't normal? Women like Jane Austen and Mother Teresa? Then I'll be abnormal, thank you."

"I didn't notice you driving the boys away at the party last night."

"What's that to do with the price of yachts? It doesn't follow logically that if I believe in women living up to their fullest potential that I can't enjoy male attention and admiration. Guys can be fun. And they're necessary for things like singing bass and making love. Although some are better at one than the other, and some, like Marco, excel at both."

"Valerie! You didn't. You wouldn't." Expressions chased themselves across her face. Surprise, curiosity, and something else I couldn't read.

"I didn't. Wouldn't is a different matter."

Teri gave me a your-mother-is-listening look and poked me under the table to make sure I got the message. (Does she imagine Amanda never heard of sex?) She said, "He doesn't like the name Marco. I call him Marc."

"Marco is exotic." I couldn't resist adding, just to see how she'd react, "And sexy."

Teri reacted exactly as I expected. "I hope you're not falling for Marc. He's much too old for you. I know he's handsome and charming, but he's—well, experienced. Mama says he's a heartbreaker, and I wouldn't want you to . . ." As usual, she left the sentence dangling.

"Are you sure you're not warning me off to keep him for yourself?"

She blushed beet red. "Me and Marc? Don't be ridiculous. He's my first cousin."

I was only trying to have the last word; I hadn't realized that Teri had a crush on her cousin. I felt sorry for her. Not because of Marco—a secret crush is fun in a sad sort of way—but because she can't help advertising her emotions to the whole world. She doesn't know how to play it cool the way I do. I said, "I was just kidding. I know you have Peter." I turned to Amanda. "Teri's boyfriend, Peter, is a scientific genius. I never understood the Doppler effect until he explained it to me."

Teri insisted that Peter wasn't her boyfriend, that they were just in the science club together. I said they were made for each other and she'd better grab him before someone else did. The waiter brought the dessert cart. Amanda had a lemon sherbet. Teri and I had a pastry-eating contest. I won by downing two éclairs, a napoleon, and a strawberry tart. Then, too stuffed to move, I watched the scenery go by.

As the yacht docked, the orchestra played "New York, New York, it's a wonderful town." People started pushing back their chairs and gathering up their things. I was in no hurry to leave. I was content to nibble a last cookie and watch those people who always have to be the first ones in or out making a mad dash for the exit.

The uniformed flunky suddenly appeared at my side. He asked Amanda, "Ready to leave?" Then, without giving me a chance to protest, he pulled me away from the table. The sudden switch from being a person enjoying my birthday brunch to being a thing wheeled around at some flunky's whim was horrible. But there was nothing I could do about it. There was no way I could get down that gangplank by myself. So I hunched down in my chair as if I were totally paralyzed and let him push me across the room. Amanda and Teri followed us.

When people blocked the way, the flunky called out in a voice that carried across the river to New Jersey, "Please let the little lady through."

Being pushed through the aisle that opened for me was worse than walking barefoot over hot coals. I wanted to die. But no matter how much you want to, you don't actually die of shame. I stared miserably down at my feet in their high-heeled shoes (feet that looked so normal) to avoid the pity-the-poor-cripple glances of the other diners.

The journey across the room and down the gangplank

took a thousand years. Somewhere around year 500, my shame and misery turned to anger. I was sure the effing flunky was enjoying bumping me down the effing gangplank while he showed off to the world that he was taking part in Be-Kind-to-the-Disabled Week. I ground my teeth in helpless rage.

When we were finally on dry land, he gave my wheelchair to Amanda like a supermarket packer handing over the grocery bags. Then he told her he hoped she'd had a good time and would come again. He didn't say anything to me. The whole time he'd been pushing me around, he never addressed a single word to me. He never even looked directly at me. To keep even a shred of my tattered self-respect, I had to show him that I counted.

So I kicked him.

Of course, my foot never connected. The flunky walked away without feeling anything. But I felt something strange. When I realized what it was, I screamed, "My leg moved! Did you see? It moved!"

Amanda and Teri looked at my still leg. Breathlessly, I explained, "That guy made me so mad treating me as if I didn't exist, as if I was just some thing to lug around, that I wanted to kick him. I automatically kicked with my *right leg*, and it moved! Not a lot. But it definitely moved. I felt it."

They both got so excited that neither of them mentioned that kicking flunkies isn't the polite thing to do. They both said how wonderful it was that I'd finally been able to move the leg. Amanda said she'd told me I was getting some return, and Teri said she'd told me bad patients get better faster.

On the way home in the limousine, after we'd calmed down, Amanda said, "Try it again."

"You mean kick my leg again?" I was ashamed to admit that I was terrified to try. So I tried to kick. Actually, I tried to try, but my body had forgotten how.

My shoulders moved. My arms moved. My good leg moved. The bad leg stayed as still as a shoe-store display.

Amanda said, "It may take a while before you can move at will. But if you did it once, you'll be able to do it again."

I said, "Sure."

Teri said, "Your leg's probably just tired."

I said, "Sure."

I thought, they were in back of me. They didn't see the leg move. Maybe I imagined it.

11

Teri

Mama had the baby.

It wasn't at all like in the movies where the mother is wheeled away as soon as she gets to the hospital and the family paces up and down worrying in the waiting room. Rosanne said that was old-fashioned. She told Mama that nowadays hospitals have birthing rooms where the father stays with the mother the whole time and encourages her. Mama said she never heard of a man being around when a baby was born, but Rosanne said what was the use of having a daughter who was training to be a nurse if you didn't take her advice. So Mama said it was all right with her if Rosanne could convince Papa, and Papa surprised us by agreeing right away.

So Rosanne and I sat home trying to watch TV while Papa was in the birthing room holding Mama's hand. I was too worried and excited to pay attention to the screen. Worried because what if something happened to Mama. Excited at having a baby to cuddle and play with.

The phone rang in the middle of "The Simpsons" and Rosanne and I bumped into each other running to get it. I let Rosanne answer because she's the oldest.

She yelled, "It's a boy!" and danced around the room with the phone for a partner. I tried to wait patiently while she asked a lot of nurse-type questions. Finally, she told me everything was fine and let me talk to Papa.

Papa sounded so happy and proud when he said, "Now my family is complete. I have a son."

Papa let me talk to Mama. Mama sounded happy and tired. "Your little brother is lying on my stomach. He's so handsome. He's going to break all the girls' hearts when he grows up."

"Like Marc."

"Like your papa. He was the handsomest man on Mulberry Street. Every girl in the neighborhood was after him. At our engagement party, one girl who wouldn't give up danced with him like he was the wall and she was the wallpaper." She giggled like a teenager. "It didn't do her any good. He married me."

Mama never told me that story before. It made me feel special to have her share it with me. "I'm glad Papa married you. I wouldn't want any mother but you. And I promise to be a big help when you bring the baby home."

When Mama said, "Teresa, you're a good girl," my eyes filled up with tears.

Just then, the nurse came in to weigh the baby. I guess he didn't like being taken away from Mama, because he howled. Mama said, "Listen to him. What strong lungs!"

Then I really started to cry. Happy crying. Because an hour ago there was no such person as Anthony D'Angelo,

Jr., and now he was telling the world what he wanted and didn't want. It was a miracle.

"If a miracle goes on awhile," I told Valerie, "it stops being so miraculous."

She didn't answer. She was doing math homework on a calculator that gave a little *ping* every time she tapped a key. The pinging was fine thanks for my dropping everything when Valerie's mother called to say she was worried about Valerie being so depressed about her leg still barely moving that she had hardly gone out of the house except to the center since the birthday brunch. Valerie's mother said some company might help. So I came running. And ended up listening to *ping ping.*

I said, "We're not allowed to use calculators in school. Sister Josephine says unnecessary reliance on machines softens our bodies and brains."

"I don't go to school. I have home instruction. And my brain is quite solid, thank you." She hit another key. *Ping.*

"I guess I'll go home and work on my science project. There's no sense hanging around trying to talk to somebody who isn't listening."

"I was listening."

"You weren't. You were banging on that thing."

"I can do two things at once. I heard you. You said you were tired of having the baby around."

"I didn't!"

"Then what's eating you?"

"I *like* having the baby around. When I hold him on my shoulder and pat his little back, he cuddles into me and I melt like an ice cream cone in the sun. What's eating me is I almost never get to hold him. I can hardly get near him. Either my aunts are crowding around his crib, or Mama's nursing him and Rosanne's telling me not to interrupt, or Papa's bouncing him on his lap, or Rosanne's bathing and dressing him. Mama's forgotten that when she was sick last summer and Rosanne was away, *I* took care of her. Now that Rosanne is home, she gives Mama advice like Mama never had a baby before. Mama listens to Rosanne, but if I suggest something, neither of them pays any attention. Rosanne gets to bathe Little Tony and feed him his relief bottle. I don't even get to change a dirty diaper. If I packed my things and moved out, it'd be a month before anyone noticed I was gone."

"Actually, it's normal to be jealous."

I'd expected Valerie to be on my side. I'd hoped she would come up with some terrific idea to stop everyone shutting me out. But she'd made up her mind that she knew more about how I felt than I did. Sometimes when she did that she was right, and I discovered there was more to me than I thought. But this time she was wrong. I insisted, "I just told you I'm not jealous."

She just gave me the green-eyed stare.

I'd had all I could take of people acting superior to me. I said, "You're a great one to tell me what's wrong with me. You carried on so about not going back to school that the doctor gave you a note for home instruction. Now you just hide in the house feeling sorry for yourself."

"You're remarkably well informed."

"Your mother . . ." I clapped my hand to my mouth.

It was too late. Valerie said with deadly calm, "So Amanda asked you to visit."

"I meant to come anyway. Except with the baby and

my science project and everything . . . You've got to see the project. It's a solar house."

"Get out."

I laughed nervously. "That's what you said the day we met. Remember when I came into your room in the hospital?"

"If you enjoy paying pity visits to poor cripples, if it makes you feel bloody superior, I'll give you a list. Go see Lulu; you'll love her spitting on you. Just leave me alone. Get out and don't ever come back."

She couldn't mean it. She was supposed to be so smart. How could she not know that I came because I was her friend? Why, she was the first person I called when Little Tony was born. I stammered, "I'm sorry if I hurt your feelings."

She didn't hear me because she was yelling, "Get out or I'll throw you out!" She grabbed her crutches and started to pull herself out of the wheelchair.

She was so clumsy I was terrified she'd fall and hurt herself again. I cried, "Sit down! I'm going."

I waited till she was safely back in her chair before I left.

I stood out in the hall staring at the apartment door, hesitating about going back in and telling Valerie to stop being so silly. Okay, I shouldn't have said that about her hiding in the house, but she'd said worse to me lots of times. And I'd have come to see her even if Amanda didn't ask. Hadn't I kept phoning even though Valerie never bothered to call me? She didn't even call to say thanks when I sent her the pictures Rosanne took at our double birthday party. No, I had to call her to find out if she got them. Now *she* was mad at *me*. Well, if that's all Valerie

85

cared about our friendship, I wasn't going to worry about it. I didn't care.

I jabbed the elevator button. When the elevator didn't come right away, I ran down the five flights of stairs. I practically ran the whole way home. Rosanne says exercise helps when you're upset, but it didn't help me. I still felt like my best friend died.

Mama and Rosanne were giving Little Tony a bath when I got home. Rosanne has lots of special things for the baby's bath: cotton balls to wipe his eyes, Q-Tips to clean his ears, a soft brush to stimulate his scalp. She didn't notice me come in.

I waited till Little Tony was dried and dressed before I asked Mama, "Can I take him for a walk in his carriage?"

Rosanne answered for her. "It's too soon after his bath."

"I'll wait awhile."

Rosanne said, "You won't be able to manage the carriage alone. I'll have to go along."

Suddenly I knew why Valerie curses. It would've cooled my heart to spit out a mouthful of *bloody*s and *effing*s. But I just said quietly, "He's my brother too."

Mama looked at me like she was trying to read something written on my forehead. Then she said, "Take him now while it's still warm out. Have a nice walk."

I managed the carriage just fine alone. I strolled down Broadway. Whenever I stopped to look in a store window, some woman was sure to peek into the carriage and smile. Once an old lady asked, "Is it a boy or girl?" even though he had a blue blanket and a ribbon on the pillow that said *Anthony, Jr.* But she was old, so I smiled and answered, "A boy."

But even while I was enjoying having Little Tony all to

myself, the way Valerie treated me was nagging at me. When I left to visit Valerie this morning, Mama said to invite her to see the baby. Mama wouldn't be so quick with her invitation if she knew how mean and selfish Valerie was. Mama'd keep Valerie miles away from Little Tony so she wouldn't contaminate him.

The baby started to whimper and I crossed over to the island, sat down on the bench, and picked him up. He stopped crying and lay against me all warm and cuddly. I sang him the Italian lullaby Mama sings.

Then I put him on his back on my lap. He stared up at me with wide-open eyes. A woman sitting on the bench next to me said, "He's learning to recognize you."

"Do you really think so? He's only a month old."

"He's big for a month. And beautiful."

I bragged, "He was eight pounds, eleven ounces when he was born, and he looks like his papa."

The woman made goo-goo noises. Then she got up, telling me, "Take good care of your child, and he'll bring you joy."

When she was gone, I said to Little Tony, "She thought I was your mother. She doesn't think I'm too young to take care of you. She doesn't think I'm too young for anybody to listen to me. Too bad Mama and Rosanne didn't hear her."

He smiled. His very first smile, and I was the one to see it. "Just wait till I tell Rosanne you smiled. She'll say it was gas or something, but you and me know better, don't we?"

I waited for another smile, but it was one to a customer. I begged, "One more, please," but he just stared at me. He must've taken staring lessons from Valerie.

"About Valerie. I feel sort of like I lost a part of myself I didn't know I had till I met her. I'll bet she feels bad too. She needs me. Her mother said so. And her mother practically admitted that Valerie acts mean and selfish when she's unhappy. But after the way Valerie treated me, I can't just go crawling back, can I? Not even if she did it because she's miserable. Still, I have to do something. But what?"

Little Tony closed his eyes, leaving me to figure it out for myself.

I'm terrible at plotting. But, as Sister Josephine says, necessity is the mother of invention. When it's important, you find a way. By the time I brought the baby home and handed him over to Mama, I had an idea.

Since I don't have a phone in my room like Valerie, I had to wait till after dinner. I dawdled doing the dishes till Mama and Rosanne were in the baby's room and Papa was watching TV. Then I picked up the kitchen phone. As usual, nobody was paying any attention to me, but I double-checked that they couldn't hear before I dialed Aunt Flo's number.

Aunt Flo said she noticed I wore the necklace she gave me for my birthday to Little Tony's christening. I was so glad to have somebody notice something about me that I chatted with her for quite a while before I asked if Marc was home.

Marc said, "Hi, Coz, what's doing?"

"Will you do me a favor?"

"Anything for my favorite cousin. Perfume from Paris. Diamonds from King Solomon's mines. Or do you want me to break someone's legs?"

Uptight as I was, I couldn't help giggling. Then, before

I lost my nerve, I asked, "Will you call Valerie like I don't know about it and take her for a drive and while you're out say you want to drop in to see Little Tony?"

"Want to tell me why?"

Even though I was embarrassed to tell him, I was afraid he'd refuse if I didn't explain. "Valerie got it into her head that I feel sorry for her because of her leg, and so she got mad, which means she's really upset, and I don't want her to be upset, but if I call her she'll probably hang up, and her mother says Valerie needs to get out and see people and . . ."

"I get the idea."

Hearing the laughter in his voice, I said stiffly, "It's okay if you don't want to."

"Hey, what are cousins for? Friday evening okay?"

"Great."

"Of course, Valerie might not want to go driving with me."

"No girl can resist you."

This time he laughed out loud.

When Marc hung up, I sat at the kitchen table eating a big piece of cake and congratulated myself on being so clever. My plot was going to work. Marc and Valerie would drop in and Mama would insist on feeding them, and while we were sitting around the kitchen table Valerie would realize how stupid she'd acted and she'd apologize. . . . Well, knowing Valerie, she wouldn't exactly apologize, but we'd be friends again.

I wiped the cake crumbs off the tablecloth. Why does Mama have to use a plastic tablecloth? Valerie's mother has quilted place mats on an oak table. Valerie's mother has modern furniture and track lighting and lots of pictures and plants. I didn't realize how dark and dreary our apartment was before I saw Valerie's. When Valerie was here before, the party decorations livened things up. Now everything looked so dowdy.

Since there was no way to get Mama to buy new furniture before Friday, I could only hope that Valerie wouldn't notice. And hope that Papa wouldn't be slumped in front of the TV in his undershirt when Valerie came. Hope the baby wouldn't start screaming. I'd die of embarrassment if Mama pulled up her blouse and nursed Little Tony in front of Valerie.

12

Valerie

—

*I*t was Friday. Actually, Mrs. Go said it was Friday. I wouldn't know if she were lying; the days were all the same. Amanda left, Mrs. Go came, Mrs. Go gave me breakfast, I left most of it, the home instruction teacher came, the home instruction teacher left, Mrs. Go gave me lunch, I left most of it, she asked did I want to play gin rummy, I said I had studying.

Mrs. Go came in with my brace. "I'll put this on for you now. The ambulette will be here soon."

If the ambulette was coming, it probably was Friday. I pretended I was reading the book the home instructor had left.

Mrs. Go recognizes a brick wall when she runs into one. Propping my brace and crutches across my wheelchair, she pushed me out of the apartment, in and out of the elevator, and across the sidewalk to the ambulette. I didn't make a move to help.

Something was missing from the ambulette. Actually, someone. I asked, "Where's Lulu?"

Derek answered, "She's in the hospital."

As if I weren't low enough, now I had to feel like a witch for being disgusted by Lulu, for secretly believing she could stop shaking and spitting if she made an effort to act normal. I couldn't bring myself to ask how serious it was.

He told me anyway. "She had a bad seizure, and they put her in the hospital for tests. Lulu's different from us. With a little luck and a lot of hard work, we might improve. Lulu has a progressive disease. All she can hope for is to slow it down."

"Must we keep talking about it?" I couldn't bear to imagine how Lulu felt lying in the hospital knowing that nothing the doctors did would stop her getting worse and worse. I didn't want to think about Lulu, hospitals, progressive diseases, or paralyzed legs.

"Sorry. I forgot how long it takes to get used to it."

"I'll never get used to it!"

"You think you won't, but you will."

There's no answer to stupidity. I turned away.

It wasn't my day. No day is, but today earned the booby prize. Rob started in on me when I got to P.T. "The blisters on your foot are healed, but no callus has formed. That means you're not practicing on your crutches every day."

So I wasn't. So what.

"You've gradually stopped working here too. Last month you couldn't wait to get onto crutches. Now you expect me to do your therapy for you."

Tough. That's what he gets paid for.

92

"When someone has a serious accident, her body isn't the only thing injured. Her spirit is hurt also. She feels angry and depressed. Here at the center, we have a team approach . . ."

"No! I won't talk to your bloody psychiatrist."

"You're one step ahead of me. You'd think a girl clever enough to know what I was about to suggest would also be bright enough to accept help."

I said bitterly, "You all want to *help* me. It never occurs to you that I'm sick of being helped, that I don't want your effing help."

"What do you want?"

I wanted my leg back. I wanted to be whole again. I wanted to be myself again. Since there was no way I could say that, I just shook my head.

He asked gently, "Do you want to learn to put your brace on by yourself?"

"I hate the effing brace. But what difference does it make what a helpless cripple wants?"

"You might want to try walking in the bars without the brace and see what happens."

Struggling down the bars without the brace was even more terrifying than the first time I tried it with the brace on. Although I leaned most of my weight on my arms, the leg threatened to collapse under me. Rob stayed close in case it did. But my leg held. And I discovered I could bend my knee a little if I concentrated. I concentrated so hard that I was dripping sweat by the time I made it to the end. Rob said it was enough for now and made me sit and rest. I noticed he was sweaty too. And he didn't mention the psychiatrist again.

I left P.T. feeling wonderful/awful. Wonderful because

93

for the first time since the accident, I'd stood on my own two legs and maybe, just maybe, it was the beginning of a normal life. Awful because maybe it wasn't. Awful because there was so far to go, and I was afraid to hope.

O.T. tipped the scales to awful. Eunice acted cutesier than usual (if that's possible) while we all pretended Lulu wasn't missing. I left depressed enough for two psychiatrists.

Amanda was home already. She explained that an important client was in New York, and she had to take him to dinner. She said she'd get some takeout for me. Did I want pizza, deli, or Chinese?

I said I couldn't care less, and she said she was sorry but it was unexpected. I didn't listen.

The phone rang. Amanda answered it and told me, "It's someone named Marc."

"He's Teri's cousin. Say I'm not here."

She handed me the phone. "Talk to him."

Marco said he had an errand in my neighborhood and would I like to go for a drive. I said I was too tired.

Amanda stood listening. She said, "Tell him to hold on."

I told him.

She said, "Valerie, you can't wall yourself into this house like a hermit in a cell. Tell him you'd love to go."

I told Marco, "My mother says I have to go."

He laughed. "I'm lucky your mother is on my side."

When Amanda put my brace on for me, I started to tell her about walking in the bars without it. But I was afraid she'd make it into more than it was, and we'd both be devastated if it didn't work out. Unfortunately, there's a gap as big as the Grand Canyon between managing some-

94

thing with help for five minutes in P.T. and doing it on your own all the time at home.

She opened my closet and held up an outfit for my inspection. "How about this? It should cheer you up."

"I thought you hate that because it makes me look like a fugitive from a rock group."

"I do. Isn't that why it's your favorite?"

Sometimes Amanda surprises me with what she understands. I almost asked her if she thought I was depressed. Of course I was feeling down, but wasn't that reasonable after what had happened to me? I certainly didn't need a stupid psychiatrist, but maybe . . . Then I saw Amanda checking her watch to see if she was late for her appointment. Maybe we could talk sometime when she wasn't so busy and I wasn't so depressed.

She handed me the earrings Teri gave me for my birthday. "These should complete the rock-group look."

"Fine." Why should I refuse to wear the earrings just because I was angry at Teri? Actually, I wasn't angry anymore. If Teri called to apologize, I'd forgive her. Actually, I was surprised she hadn't called yet. Not that I cared. I didn't need her. I didn't need anyone. I could manage just fine on my lonesome, thank you.

I fidgeted waiting for Marco. Although I'd never tell anyone, I'm nervous about going out. I don't have agoraphobia, a fear of open spaces. I looked up the symptoms in a psychology book, and I don't have them. I don't panic or get dizzy or break into a sweat. I just start thinking of all the terrible things that could happen to me outside. I imagine tripping over a crack in the sidewalk or being knocked down by a kid running for a ball. I imagine trying to cross the street on my crutches and a car jumping the light and slamming into me and the ambulance taking me back to the hospital. I couldn't bear being in the hospital again.

My imagination had me in a sweat by the time Marco came, but when I was actually in the street I couldn't imagine why I'd been so afraid. Marco gave me time to admire his bright red sports car before he opened the door and helped me in. He kept up a line of talk designed to impress me, complimenting my clothes and the way my hair glowed in the fading sunlight. All with a little smile that said it was just a game, but wasn't it fun. It beat gin rummy with Mrs. Go, so I played along.

We drove up to the Cloisters to see the sun set over the river. He put his arm casually around my shoulders as the sky went flaming pink and faded to lavender. Remembering Teri's talk about Marco being an experienced heartbreaker, I waited for his next move. It was tempting to imagine myself in his arms with his mouth on mine. Which, I'm sure, is exactly how all the girls who fell for him felt. But I don't like being one of the crowd. If I play a game, I like to win.

I planned my response carefully, but he never made his move. He took his arm off my shoulder to point, "There's the first star. Make a wish."

Suddenly, I'd had it with silly games. Wishing on a star wouldn't give me my leg back. I shook my head. "Thanks for the ride, but I'm terribly tired. Please take me home."

"Your wish is my command." He started the car.

We drove down Riverside Drive. When he made a left, I said, "You're turning too soon."

"I have an errand to run first. It won't take long."

Since he was driving, I was stuck waiting for him to

pick up his laundry or fill his grandmother's prescription. I closed my eyes to show how tired I was.

I opened them when the car stopped in front of Teri's house. Marco said, "I promised to bring the baby something. Come in and see him."

Did he think I couldn't add two and two without a computer? "Teri put you up to this."

"Guilty with an excuse, your honor. Teri said you two had a fight and asked me to trick you into coming. I knew you'd catch on, but I couldn't resist a chance to see you again." He slid my crutches onto my arms, picked me up, and put me on my feet.

That kind of macho move either makes you melt or want to spit. It did a bit of both to me. Acting as if I'd gotten out of the car under my own steam, I said, "If Teri wants to make up this much, I'd be a witch to refuse. Let's go see her."

As we rode up in the elevator, I prayed that Teri didn't intend to make it into a big reconciliation scene. Now that she'd made the first move, I could admit to myself that I'd missed her and wanted to be friends again. But if I had my way, we'd just act as if nothing happened.

Actually, Teri didn't get a chance for a scene or anything else because her mother rushed to greet Marco and me like long-lost relatives. She settled me into a chair and made a big fuss over me. I usually can't bear being fussed over, but she was so sincerely welcoming that I rather enjoyed it. She introduced me to all the other people in the room.

Teri interrupted her. "Mama, Valerie won't remember all their names."

When you meet new people, it's important to establish

that you're special. I said, "Yes, I will," and reeled them off. "Rosanne and Marco and your parents I already know. The blond woman is Aunt Flo. She's Marco's mother. Her husband is Uncle Charley. Aunt Paula is wearing a black dress. Mrs. Nicolosi is a neighbor. She lives on the second floor."

It's not that hard to do. The trick is making a mental image for each person. (A nickel floating on the sea for Mrs. Nicolosi.) But Teri's mother cried, "*Brava!*" before she said, "You didn't meet the most important person yet," and hurried away to fetch him.

She put the baby in my arms. He was so tiny, I was terrified of breaking him. But when Rosanne hurried over to make sure I was supporting his back and head properly, I acted as if I held two sets of twins before breakfast every day. You have to show the Rosannes of this world that you're firmly in control.

Teri's mother asked if my arms were getting tired. I shook my head. "I lift weights to strengthen them."

"I saw how you lean on your arms when you walk. I give you credit for working hard to make them strong." Then she asked did I do exercises for my legs too and did the doctors say the injured leg was getting better.

Teri interrupted, "Mama, Valerie doesn't like to talk about it."

When I said, "Only when people ask just to give me advice or tell me about their operations," Teri suddenly got very quiet.

What was bugging her? I'd come, hadn't I? And I was going out of my way to be friendly and sociable and make a good impression on her family. I was doing everything short of bursting into a great big apology to show her I was sorry I'd blown up at her. Did she expect me to push a peanut across the rug with my nose?

Teri's mother asked tons of questions about my work at the center. She was so easy to talk to, so genuinely interested and encouraging, that I told her more about what it was really like than I'd ever told anyone except Teri. Then I surprised myself by adding that I'd walked in the bars without the brace for the first time today.

Teri said, with that hurt look, "You didn't tell me that."

I asked reasonably, "How could I? I haven't seen you since then." But she still looked hurt. She has this thing about being left out or passed over. It was just like her to imagine that my feeling at home with her mother meant I was ignoring her.

Actually, Teri does kind of fade into the wallpaper while her mother comes running to take care of you. But they're really a lot alike. They both care about other people. Teri had cared enough about me to get Marco to bring me here to be friends again. So it was up to me to soothe her hurt feelings—even if they didn't make any sense.

Watching Teri out of the corner of my eye, I told her mother, "Rob wants my leg tested again, but it means sticking needles into me from my back to my toes. They did it in the hospital and it's a horror, so I'm stalling until I'm braver."

"You're a brave girl whether you take the needles or not."

"It helps to have people think so." Looking straight at Teri, I added, "It helps to have friends." But she didn't seem to know I meant her.

Teri's mother declared, "You have friends here. Come visit whenever you want. And play with the baby."

99

On cue, the baby began to howl. She said, "He's hungry. I'll take him inside and feed him. Teresa, why don't you show Valerie your science project?"

Teri obediently led me to a table set up across the room.

"A dollhouse," I exclaimed. "I love dollhouses." I consider them a total bore, but the lie was in a good cause.

She corrected me. "It's a solar house, powered by that battery of lights." She pointed to little silver tapes running across the tops of the inside walls. "The electrical system is in. The hot-water heating system is a problem. The solar collector on the roof wasn't too hard, but the pipes have to be so small . . ."

"You mean the house is actually going to have light and heat?"

"The idea is to demonstrate the uses of solar energy. I started with an old dollhouse, and Papa let me have scrap metal from the garage for the light boom."

"Teri, it's fantastic!" This time I meant it. The more I looked, the more impressed I was. I had no idea Teri could do anything like this; I was supposed to be the creative one.

Doubtfully, "Do you really think so?"

"It's bloody marvelous. The only improvement I could possibly suggest is a greenhouse to show another use of solar energy."

Finally, Teri smiled. Her face sent out all-is-forgiven signals. She said, "You always have good ideas. All I have to do to make a greenhouse is to glass in the porch."

13

Teri

⁓

I was so nervous that I kept running to the bathroom every three minutes. Only, with the family getting together at our house to go to the science competition, it was mostly occupied. Aunt Paula had to fix a run in her stocking, and Aunt Flo needed more spray on her hair, and Mama was as nervous as I was.

Mama declared, "If the judges have eyes, they'll give Teri a prize and send her project on to the citywide scholarship competition. Can you imagine her winning a college scholarship?"

Aunt Paula said, "We mustn't count our chickens before they're hatched."

Aunt Flo said, "There are five prizes, and I think Teri has a good chance to win one. With all the children in the family, I've gone to the science contests for years, and I never saw anything as good as Teri's solar house."

In spite of my nervousness, I was enjoying being the center of attention for a change. Even Rosanne was acting

101

like I was somebody special. She let me hand Little Tony to Mama to zip into his Snugli. And the way everyone was talking, I felt like I really had a chance at a prize. The solar house had come out better than I ever dreamed possible. When I looked at it, I almost couldn't believe I'd made it. Afraid of jinxing myself by taking all the credit, I told Aunt Flo, "Mama needlepointed the rugs, and Rosanne painted the tiny pictures for the walls."

Mama said, "We just dressed the house up a little. You did all the science and building parts by yourself, and that's what they judge. Think of the hours you spent at the garage making the metal stand for the lights."

Papa said, "She learned to weld so fast it's a shame she isn't a boy. I'd make her a mechanic in no time."

Mama said, "So let's go for the judging."

When we got to school, Julia and Patsy pushed through the crowd of relatives who'd come to see the projects displayed and to hear the winners announced. Patsy told me, "All the girls love your house."

Julia said, "It's a terrific project. If we were the judges, you'd win hands down."

Patsy nodded. "Better than Peter's. He's president of the science club, and he just did a report like us."

I defended Peter. "It's not just a report. It's a study of the environmental impact of the proposed West Side Highway."

Julia asked, "Where did you find such tiny potted plants for the greenhouse?"

"Valerie bought them for me. She knows stores for all kinds of unusual things." I looked around. "Marc's bringing her today. I wonder what's keeping them. I hope her leg isn't hurting. . . ." Valerie says her leg hurts when she's really too miserable to move. I'm the only one who knows she gets these awful attacks of misery where all of her feels paralyzed, not just her leg. Amanda doesn't know about them. She's relieved because Valerie goes out now. When I begged Valerie to tell her mother or Rob about the attacks, she got so mad at me that I swore on my baby brother's life not to betray her secret.

Mama said, "Valerie called while you were down using Mrs. Nicolosi's bathroom. She said she might be late because Marco's taking her to see her friend in the hospital first."

"Why didn't you tell me?"

Mama looked surprised. "I'm telling you now." But Valerie was my friend and she'd called to leave a message for *me*. Or had she? The way Mama practically adopted Valerie, maybe she was calling Mama. Or Little Tony. Valerie's crazy for Little Tony. Funny that before Valerie met my family, I was afraid she'd look down on them. I never dreamed that she'd love them and they'd love her. Or that I'd be jealous. Just a little bit jealous, of course.

Julia said, "Here come Valerie and Marc now. It looks like you made a match."

I shook my head. "Valerie told me—and you've got to promise not to repeat this—Marc hangs around because he can't believe any girl can resist him. He keeps trying to make Valerie flip out for him. When she won't, he tries harder. Valerie says it's like a game."

Julia sighed, "I've been after Marc for ages. Valerie comes along and grabs him just like that, and she doesn't even want him. I don't know what that girl has, but I wish I had some."

"Me too."

A path opened through the crowd for Valerie's crutches. She looked white and shaken. Without even stopping to kiss or tickle the baby, she told us in a hoarse voice, "Lulu is so sick, I think she's dying."

Rosanne was immediately the nurse. "It's hard for an outsider to judge how sick a patient is. You're probably worrying for nothing."

Valerie gave Rosanne a look, and Rosanne let it go. I've tried practicing Valerie's looks in the bathroom mirror, but they don't work for me.

Marc, who didn't look too good himself, said, "Valerie's mother thinks she shouldn't go to the hospital because it upsets her."

Rosanne suggested, "Call or send a card instead."

Valerie wasn't having any. "I'm going, and nobody can stop me! I'd visit Lulu every day if I could get there. I owe it to her." Then she suddenly got cheerful. "Enough of that. I came to admire Teri's house. Where is it?" Nobody but me seemed to notice that she was too cheery.

After double-checking that everything in my house was in place, she asked Peter to show her which projects might compete with it. I trailed after her and Peter as she examined the other projects so carefully that you'd think she was the official judge. Then she said if there was any justice in this world, my solar house was on its way to the city competition.

So why did I need to go the bathroom when Sister Josephine took the microphone to announce the prizes?

Sister Josephine cleared her throat. There was silence. "The fifth prize goes to . . ." She was doing it like the

Miss America contest, leaving the best for last. "Peter Blake."

She went on to describe Peter's environmental study. I was clapping so hard I didn't hear. I was so happy for Peter. And since I secretly felt that a working solar house outclassed a report no matter how good the report was. . . .

Sister Josephine tapped the microphone. "Fourth prize . . ." I wasn't greedy. I'd be happy with fourth. I'd be thrilled. She announced, "Christopher Spina."

I clapped for Christopher because he's Patsy's cousin. Besides, if Christopher got fourth prize, maybe I'd get third. Valerie examined every slide Christopher made before she said they were good but my house was better, and Peter agreed with her. Third prize would be worth all my work—including having to make up the homework I'd skipped to have time for it.

"Third prize is awarded to Kevin Murphy."

Second prize was next. I was so nervous I practically wet my pants. I held my breath and prayed. Second prize went to Craig Werner.

Sister Josephine tapped the microphone and cleared her throat to announce the first prize. I couldn't breathe. I felt like I was drowning. Could I possibly win first prize? Sweet Jesus, please let it be me. Please. Please.

"Matthew Young!"

I managed to clap politely—like a good loser. How could I have thought I'd ever be anything but a loser? I was out of my mind to carry on all these weeks like my project was so special. Even worse than losing was being stupid enough to believe that I had what it takes to win. Me, who never even got my compositions put on the bulletin board in grade school.

When the applause died down, Sister Josephine announced, "We have three honorable mentions: Teresa D'Angelo, James Bailey, and Edward Hernandez."

It didn't register till the whole family started hugging and kissing me and telling me how proud they were. Then all I could think of was how bad I had to go to the bathroom.

I ran. When I got back, people were leaving and Sister Josephine was calling for attention. "All students who have not been awarded prizes, take your projects home today."

Rosanne started organizing. "If Marc drives Mama and the baby home, Papa can put Teri's project in our backseat."

I interrupted, "Sister Josephine didn't say anything about honorable mentions." It was finally sinking in that I'd done it. For the first time in my life, I'd won something. And what a something. Out of all these science projects, *mine* displayed a red sticker that said *First Honorable Mention*. I couldn't just pack it up and take it home. I wanted to hug my honorable mention in my arms and dance around the room with it.

Valerie said, "Actually, honorable mention and a token will get you on any subway."

Mama scolded, "Valerie! That's not nice. Honorable mention is something to be proud of."

"Not if you deserve a prize."

Mama looked at Rosanne. Rosanne is the family authority on academic things. She said, "I didn't want to say it before because the family was so enthusiastic and Teri's house was so good that you never know, but I don't remember a girl ever winning a prize. Especially not a girl who's only a sophomore. The prizes always go to seniors. Senior boys."

Mama said, "That's not fair. There should be a rule."

Peter came over in time to hear. He said, "There are rules. The citywide competition is judged on a rating scale for research, originality, and craftsmanship. The schools are supposed to use the same scale in choosing projects to send to the city. We have a copy of the rules at the science club. They don't give preference to boys or seniors."

Mama said, "Well then!"

Rosanne said, "But the judges have already decided."

Valerie ignored Rosanne. She asked Peter, "In your judgment as president of the science club, using the rating scale, did Teri deserve a prize?"

Peter thought it over carefully before he answered, "Yes."

"Would you say that she's been discriminated against?"

He thought again. "I'd say that."

"Then would you sign a petition, as science club president, to send Teri's project to the city competition? Along with the other prize winners, of course."

Where did Valerie get her ideas? Maybe petitions were the thing done at Hunter High, but not at Our Lady. If someone handed Sister Josephine a petition, she'd chop the person up into little pieces and feed her to the pigeons.

To my amazement, Peter said, "I'd be glad to sign." Shy, quiet Peter going along with such a far-out idea!

That was all Valerie needed. "I'll print the petitions on my computer, and Peter will get the science club members and the other winners to sign, and Teri can ask her friends."

I had to stop Valerie before she went any further. I was happy with my honorable mention. Very happy. It didn't give me a chance at a college scholarship, but that was such a long shot anyway. I didn't even know what I'd do with a scholarship. Valerie had this idea that I should study engineering at some fancy university in Massachusetts that cost a zillion dollars a year. But even if I won ten scholarships, I wasn't smart enough or dedicated enough for that. I didn't even know exactly what an engineer does.

I opened my mouth to tell Valerie to drop the petition idea. Somehow no words came out.

Rosanne spoke for me. She told Valerie flatly, "It won't work."

Valerie didn't even hear because she'd already pulled out a little leather notebook and started writing the petition. Mama was the one who asked Rosanne, "Why wouldn't it work?"

"Mama! You're not seriously suggesting that Teri should go around asking people to sign a petition to give her science project a prize?"

"Why shouldn't she if she wants to?"

"For one thing, nobody would sign. And even if they did, Sister Josephine would ignore it. For another, Teri isn't capable of doing such a thing. I don't want to sound mean, but Teri shakes if somebody says 'boo' to her."

If Rosanne didn't want to sound mean, then why did she? But she was right about one thing. I didn't have the guts.

Then everybody rushed to get into the act. I stood there like a dummy, like it was their project and not mine, while everyone talked. Marc thought I should take a stab at the petition, and Julia agreed with him. Patsy wasn't sure.

Aunt Paula is always sure: her position was that petitions are subversive and immoral. Aunt Flo said it was different when you were discriminated against. Julia said the real reason I didn't get a prize was because I was a girl and Patsy said in that case she'd sign. Aunt Paula said children should learn that you had to accept things in this life. Papa said we didn't want the school taking it out on me. Mama said nuns wouldn't do that. Rosanne said she knew one nun who would. Marc said it was time somebody stood up to Sister Josephine. Rosanne said I wasn't the standing-up type. Patsy said not to talk so loud because Sister Josephine might hear. Uncle Charley said to tell him whether we were taking the project home because he wanted to go outside and smoke his cigar. I stood there wishing I could flip a switch to shut them all up.

From where she was sitting, Valerie waved her crutch for quiet. The same people who'd forgotten I was there stopped talking and paid attention. Maybe they were being nice to Valerie because she's disabled, but I don't think so. There are some people in this world who get paid attention to, and some who don't.

Valerie read out what she'd written: "We the under-signed feel that Teresa D'Angelo's science project has been discriminated against in the awarding of prizes on both a sex and class basis. We strongly urge that restitution be made by including her solar house with the projects submitted to the citywide competition."

Aunt Flo thought the language should be plainer, and Julia thought the discrimination part should be stronger because that was the whole point, and Rosanne and Aunt Paula were against it no matter what the language.

I said, "Enough!"

It came out louder than I meant. Everyone stopped talking and looked at me. Including some people packing up a project at the next table.

I asked, "Shouldn't I be the one to decide?"

What I meant was: Everybody always tells me what to do because I'm the kind of person who gets pushed around. I was surprised when Mama answered like it was a real question, "It's your decision, Teresa," and Aunt Flo and Marc and Julia and Patsy nodded. Here I was too upset to open my mouth because everybody was running my life, and it turned out that all I had to do was speak up and they'd listen.

So what was I going to say?

Sometimes you have to talk to find out what you feel. I began, "Getting honorable mention means I'm somebody special. I was happy with it until . . ." I looked at Valerie. She made a gesture of tearing up the petition. Which meant I was on my own. I stumbled on, "Maybe Rosanne's right and I couldn't stand up to Sister Josephine. . . . But if I really deserve a prize . . . I mean, discrimination isn't fair. Even if that's the way it's always been." It was a relief when the baby's crying interrupted me.

Papa took him from Mama. "Give me my boy. He'll stop crying for me."

I looked at Papa bouncing Little Tony. I don't remember Papa ever playing with me like that when I was little. And if Tony grew up to be mechanical like me, Papa would give him a job in the garage in a minute.

Suddenly the words came rushing out of me. "Girls are as good as boys even if Sister Josephine and other people

110

don't think so. And if a petition is the only way to prove that . . ."

Marc said, "Good girl."

Rosanne said, "I hope you know what you're doing."

Valerie said, "Come over tomorrow and I'll print up the petition on my computer." She looked so approving that I was glad I decided to do it for her.

Decided? For her? Or for me?

I don't know how I got myself into the petition business. I really don't.

14

Valerie

—◆—

*T*he despair attacks are getting worse. I don't actually mean worse—they're already the worst anything can be—but more frequent. If I want to be a writer, I should use words that precisely express what I want to say. If I want to be a writer. If I know what I want to say.

All through the science competition, through my rooting for Teri and sweating out the judging, through my anger at that sanctimonious (how's that for a precise word?) nun for discriminating against Teri, even while I was writing the petition, I was fighting off the despair. That evening I had a terrible attack. The despair was so bad that I couldn't move; I just sat in my wheelchair like a block of wood. When it finally lifted a little, I wrote a story about a girl who loses the use of her legs, her arms, and finally her whole body, until nothing is left but her eyelids and her brain. I wrote all evening and deep into the night.

I showed the story to my home instruction teacher. (Not

the regular idiot who comes every day; the twice-a-week special for math and literature. The special has some brains.) She said, "You can't seem to decide how your character feels about her illness. One moment she is all brave acceptance and the next she is considering suicide."

Why did she expect a character in a story to be all of a piece when real people aren't? Or are they? Maybe people with whole bodies are consistent. I can't remember what I was like before the accident split me into two people in the same broken body—one person struggling fiercely to show the world she's normal, while her other self submits helplessly to attacks of despair. I said, "Forget the story. Let's do math."

When we finished, the special said, "Since Thursday is our last time, for homework make a list of what you need to review before you go back to school."

"What!"

"Go through the math book as far as we've covered and list anything you have questions about."

I know how to make an effing list; what I didn't know was where she got the stupid idea I was going back to school. When I finally got that through to her, she told me that the three months of home instruction my doctor had authorized were up this week, and my regular teacher should have discussed it with me because I was his case.

"I don't care whose bloody case I am. I'm not going back to school."

"It's normal to feel insecure about returning. But it's like diving into a swimming pool; after the first shock, you discover that the water is quite warm."

After the first shock, I discovered that I was shaking. I felt cold and weak all over. I reached for the phone, trying to hide the trembling in my hand and keep my voice steady. "I'd better discuss this with my mother. Don't let me make you late for your next appointment."

By the time I got through to Amanda, my weakness had turned back to anger. I told Amanda what the idiot teacher had said and demanded, "How am I supposed to go back to school? Fly? Drop by parachute into a classroom where I won't have the foggiest idea what's going on?"

She promised to look into it immediately.

I nursed my anger until Amanda came home to report, "To continue home instruction, you need another doctor's note saying that you are still unable to attend school for either physical or emotional reasons. I called the doctor, who said that he relies on the physical therapist's opinion. So I called Rob. Rob thinks that returning to school will speed your physical recovery by forcing you to walk more. But he said if there are emotional reasons for you to stay home, he can arrange an appointment with the center psychiatrist."

That fink! Lulling me into believing he'd given up on the psychiatrist while he was biding his time like a cat posted outside a mousehole. I'd show him he'd picked the wrong mouse. "Rob has psychiatrists on the brain. He yells for one if someone's too tired to work in P.T. Or panics for a minute about going back to school. My teacher said it's normal to be nervous. It's like diving into a swimming pool—scary while you're teetering on the board, but once you take the plunge, the water's fine." I went on to say that now that I thought about it, I could see that going back to school would exercise the leg, challenge my mind, et cetera.

114

I expected her to give me a you-can't-fool-your-mother look and ask, "What's really going on?"

Instead she said, "I was troubled by Rob's attitude. Until I spoke to him, I felt that you were starting to cope well. You no longer hide in your room and you've made new friends. However, if you've confided in Rob . . ."

Knowing Teri has made me an expert on dangling sentences. Leaving a sentence hanging either means (1) there is something you don't want to say, or (2) there is something you don't want to hear. As surely as if it were printed in bold black letters on TV prompt cards, I knew that Amanda didn't want to hear from the part of me who wasn't "coping well."

There are times you have to be a parent to your parent. I told her (truthfully), "I don't confide in Rob. Actually, I'm too busy grunting and sweating to talk to him."

"Valerie, if you're not comfortable about returning to school, for any reason whatsoever . . ."

Again a dangling sentence. She didn't want to hear that it wasn't just school, that it was everything, that I couldn't cope with being a cripple, that I didn't want to cope, that I welcomed the despair and hugged it to me like a teddy bear, that I was ashamed of the despair because compared to Lulu or even Derek I was lucky. Only I didn't feel lucky. Life had kicked my legs out from under me, and I wanted to lie where I'd fallen and moan.

I couldn't blame Amanda for not wanting to hear that garbage. Self-pity is disgusting. "I said I don't mind going back to school. The problem is getting there."

She smiled, pulling a rabbit out of a hat. "There's a special school bus, but knowing how you feel about such

115

things, I called the limousine company. They'll drive you to school."

"In a *limo*?"

"They also have private cars and minibuses. You might start with a car and switch to a minibus when you get stronger."

She was trying so hard to make it right for me. I said, "You must've been on the phone all afternoon."

"The office can spare me for a few hours." But I could see she was pleased that I appreciated all her effort.

"Can I take a car to the center too? I hate the ambulette."

"Certainly, since you'll go directly from school to the center. We'll just add the trip home to your father's bill. I called him after I spoke to the limousine people, and he agreed to pay for the car."

It was my day to get clobbered without warning. "I thought Dad was in England on business. When did he get back?"

"A week or two ago. When I spoke to him today, he said to tell you he hasn't forgotten about the Thai restaurant. He said he'd call you soon."

"He'll call when the effing moon turns blue."

"Valerie, don't talk like that."

"Why shouldn't I?"

"Because he's your father and he loves you."

Amanda tries so hard not to involve me in her bitterness at Dad that she bends over backward to give him the benefit of the doubt. Even when there is no doubt. Dad promised me that after the divorce we'd go out to dinner— just the two of us—every week or so. Ha! The last time was right after my birthday. I remember because I wore the diamond earrings he sent for a birthday present. (For two cents, I'd flush the effing things down the toilet.) We ate Japanese, and he promised to take me for Thai food before he left for England. He didn't. Now he had been back for two weeks, and he still hadn't called. I said, "I'm hungry. What's for dinner?"

"Tuna salad. Why don't you call your father while I'm making it?"

No way. "I have to call Teri to find out what happened with the petition." I picked up the phone. If Dad decided to call me, let him get a busy signal. "Three will get you five she didn't have the nerve to show it to anyone."

Teri answered the phone with, "Valerie, I was just going to call you. I got nineteen signatures! The picture of the solar house your computer did on the petition was so cute I took it to school today to show Julia in the cafeteria. She signed the petition and passed it around the table, and one of the girls took it to a friend at a different table, and she took it to another table, and by the time it came back to me the whole page was filled. Want to come over and see it? Papa could pick you up, and you could have supper."

"I'd better not. I go back to school next week, and I'm supposed to make a list of things to review before then."

"Back to school? That's great!"

"Sure."

"You don't sound too happy about it."

"Are you happy about bucking Sister Josephine?"

"But I'm terrified of Sister Josephine." There was a pause. I could almost hear her figuring it out. Then, "I can't believe you're scared to go back to school. I mean, the only reason I let Julia pass the petition around was because I was ashamed to face you if I didn't. You're always so brave."

"Not always."

"Then you shouldn't act like you are. It's hard on other people. If I knew you were scared of things too, then I wouldn't feel like such a wimp because I kept expecting Sister Josephine to jump out of nowhere and catch me with the petition and tear it up."

There's logic for you: It's wrong for me to act brave because it makes her seem cowardly in contrast. Trust Teri to dream up something like that. I told her she wasn't making any bloody sense. She gave me her you-can-out-talk-me-but-I-know-I'm-right sigh.

Then she asked, "Sure you won't come for supper? Mama's making calamari. The tentacles look yucky, but they're good."

"Dad once took me to an Italian restaurant on Arthur Avenue for calamari and I loved them, so maybe I will come." And let Dad find me out when he called. "Actually, I have a present for the baby."

"What is it?"

"You'll see." There had been a fund-raising sale in the center lobby with a woman painting messages on sweatshirts. I'd bought the tiniest size for Little Tony and had her write *My sister Teri loves me* on it. Maybe it would cheer me up to see the smile on Teri's face when I gave it to her.

15

Teri

~

I was a celebrity in school. Me, the one who never raises my hand in class because maybe my answer isn't right or my question is stupid. Me, the quiet one who nobody ever notices. All of a sudden, everybody knew me and my petition. My table in the cafeteria was like election headquarters in the beginning of November. People kept coming over to ask how many signatures I had and when was I going to present the petition. They gave me advice: Hand the petition to the principal; send it directly to the city science competition; call the Catholic archdiocese, the school board, the American Civil Liberties Union.

I discovered it was fun being an important person. I got bolder. I carried the petition with me and stopped people in the school yard, in the cafeteria, on the bus, everywhere except in class with the teacher watching. The first few times, my heart was in my mouth. After I got the hang of it, I enjoyed myself.

By Thursday evening, I was able to tell Valerie on the

phone, "I covered pretty much everybody I know even slightly. Most of them signed, but you can't believe how scared some people are. Some people wouldn't put their names on a petition to save their own lives if they were facing a firing squad in the morning."

Valerie said, "You sound just like me."

I giggled. "I do, don't I? Anyway, tomorrow I'll try the locker room before gym for the girls I only see in volleyball."

The volleyball girls asked a lot of questions, and I ended up making a speech about discrimination and our God-given right of protest. It was like inside my ordinary shy self there lurked an actress who enjoyed the lights, camera, and action. I almost forgot the purpose of the petition in the excitement of getting it signed.

I got six more signatures, and my side won the volleyball game. I felt great.

That made it even more terrible when the ax fell.

History was my last class on Friday, and Valerie and I had decided I should put the petition in the principal's mailbox Monday morning. Instead of concentrating on the lesson, I was busy thinking up ideas for getting a few more signatures before my petition-carrying days were over. So, when the teacher called me up after class, I expected a lecture on paying attention.

When she told me, "Sister Josephine wants to see you in her office at eight-thirty Monday morning," it took a minute to register.

I mumbled something and ran for the bathroom. I was so scared I practically peed in my pants. How had I been stupid enough to think I could get away with being a big shot? What was I going to do now?

16

Valerie

—

I made careful plans for going back to school on Monday morning. When the special home instruction teacher saw my list of topics to review, she called her next student to say she'd be late—very late. I pressured the regular teacher to get my class schedule, room numbers, elevator pass, et cetera, ahead of time. The regular never had a "case" who checked his every move the way I did.

With my class schedule in hand, I worked out the logistics of getting from room to room with the efficiency of a general planning an invasion. With Mrs. Go's help, I tried on every pair of pants in my closet to make sure they hid the brace completely. It was enough that the crutches showed; people didn't have to know about the brace. When nothing I owned met my exacting standards, I dragged her shopping. (Unless you're desperate, don't go shopping on crutches with an old woman who can't tell aqua from blue without a magnifying glass.) I bought a knock-'em-dead outfit to wear Monday and jeans for later in the week. I made Amanda check the make and color of the car taking me to school so I wouldn't get in with a stranger by mistake.

I brought my schoolbooks in my old backpack to P.T. on Friday for Rob to show me the best way to wear the pack while balancing on crutches. I even consulted Eunice in O.T. about where to rest my crutches in the classroom so they wouldn't be noticed. (That shows how desperate I was.) I told Derek and Fran it was the last time I would be riding the ambulette with them.

My preparations were interrupted three times by anguished phone calls from Teri about Sister Josephine's summons. The first time, I explained exactly what she should say and do. The second time, I gave her the swimming pool lecture. She wailed, "I can't swim." The third time, I told her, "If I can go back to school and face the curiosity and pity of people who knew me when I was whole, then you can bloody well stand up to Sister Josephine. *Capisce?*" I've picked up a little Italian from Teri's family.

"I understand. And you're right. But you should say *capite*. *Capisce* is the formal form, and since we're friends . . ."

I let her have the last word to give her some practice in getting the best of somebody before facing Sister Josephine.

Giving Teri the be-brave-like-me bit ruled out any possibility of my chickening out. I had to cut the tags off my new clothes, put a fresh cartridge in my pen, review my math, and wait for Monday. Wait and worry about the car being late, about bringing the wrong books, about losing the rubber grip off a crutch and slipping. Wait and think up stupid things to worry about. Wait and manufacture a hundred stupid worries to form a wall against the misery and dread that lurked in back of my mind and threatened to overwhelm me.

Sunday afternoon, Amanda put down the report she was working on. "That's the third time you've repacked your books in the past half hour. You need something to distract your mind. Let's go to a movie."

"I'd rather visit Lulu." Although I'd been too busy worrying about school to think about Lulu, once the words were out I was determined to go to the hospital.

"I don't think that's such a good idea. You need to be distracted, not depressed."

How did she know what I needed? She didn't know what was going on inside of me. Nobody knew. I hardly knew myself. I threatened, "If you won't take me to the hospital, I'll ask Marco. Or Aunt Kate. Aunt Kate worries about Lulu."

Amanda's mouth tightened, and I braced myself. She was going to let me have it. Good. It would give me an excuse to make a scene. A big scene might make me feel better. But she just asked, "Aunt Kate?"

"Teri's mother. All Teri's friends call her that."

"Ah. I must drop Mrs. D'Angelo a note thanking her for her kindness to you. However, it won't be necessary for her to take you to the hospital. I'll call a cab."

Since I've known Teri, I've become an expert at recognizing hurt feelings. I didn't mean to hurt Amanda's feelings. (Making a scene is different from hurting someone; a scene isn't personal.) I'd have said I was sorry except I knew she'd ask "What for?" Like me, Amanda won't admit

123

she hurts. I suppose I could've said I was sorry for making it so hard for her to help me. I am sorry about that. I really am. But I was afraid that once I started apologizing, I wouldn't be able to stop. I was afraid I'd blurt out that I was sorry for being a burden on her and on myself, for being a failure, a misfit, a loser, a nobody.

Yesterday I started a science fiction story about a planet where language was never invented. I got stuck after the first page because I couldn't figure out how they communicated. If I ever finish the story, I'll show it to Amanda.

Being with Lulu was agony. That was the idea. While I was helping her unwrap the presents we'd brought and catching her up on the center gossip, I was putting myself in Lulu's place. Look at those vomit-green walls, I told myself. Remember how they close in on you after you've stared at them long enough. Smell the hospital odor and remember the humiliation of having to use a bedpan. Imagine yourself lying in that bed knowing that even when you finally get out of the hospital you'll come back again and again until . . .

I couldn't bring myself to finish the fantasy. Instead I told myself sternly, Look at Lulu and then have the nerve to feel sorry for yourself. Think how Lulu feels when she sees the disgust on people's faces because she can't stop shaking and spitting no matter how hard she tries. Then have the effing nerve to feel like a freak because of your brace and crutches.

I gave myself quite a lecture. It didn't work.

*   *   *

After the hospital, Amanda and I stopped at Mc-Donald's. She bought us both Big Macs and fries, although I said I wasn't hungry and she usually only eats the salads. She said, "Under the circumstances, it's either eat junk food or get drunk."

I chewed my hamburger without tasting it. I felt my eyes filling up with tears. It was a strange feeling, as if someone had turned on a faucet behind my eyeballs, as if my crying had nothing to do with me.

Amanda said, "I know. It's so sad."

I kept chewing. My eyes overflowed and the tears leaked down my cheeks. I didn't have the energy to wipe them away.

She asked, "Is there something I can do to help?"

I shook my head. The tears dripped onto my bun. I didn't deserve her help. I didn't deserve her sympathy. I wasn't crying for Lulu. I was crying for myself. Lulu was dying, and I was crying because I was too cowardly to face the stares at school tomorrow.

Amanda patted my hand.

I pulled my hand away. I deserved to be in total despair.

17

Teri

~

I stood outside Sister Josephine's office waiting for her to see me. Waiting and trying to convince myself I didn't really need to go to the bathroom. Telling myself I'd stopped at the Girls on my way in. Telling myself to think about something else.

Think about Valerie. Right now Valerie was on her way to school for the first time since her accident. Remember what she said when I called her: If she could face the pity of the kids at school, I could face Sister Josephine. She even told me what to say, and I wrote it down. Only I'd forgotten the paper, and I was too petrified to remember what was on it. I think some stuff about the First Amendment and the constitutional rights of the individual in a democracy.

After keeping me waiting till I was practically jumping out of my skin, Sister Josephine gave me exactly one minute of her time. I didn't get a chance to use any of Valerie's arguments even if I could've remembered them. Sister

Josephine did all the talking. "It has come to my attention that you are circulating a personal petition among the students. This is a school, not a political convention. You will immediately stop all such activities on the school grounds or on school time. I have also been informed that you have fallen behind on your homework assignments. All assignments, along with notes of apology for tardiness, will be completed and handed to your teachers by Friday. You may go now."

I fled the office thanking the saints in heaven for my getting off so easy. I had already started making up the homework, and the apologies were no big deal. As for the petition, I never expected anything from it in the first place. Even if by some miracle it convinced the principal to send my project to the city competition, I couldn't believe I had a prayer of winning a scholarship.

Actually, I didn't get involved with the petition for the scholarship. I did it because . . .

Even after it was all over, I still couldn't figure out why I did it. To prove to Valerie I wasn't a wimp? To show Rosanne she didn't know everything? Maybe I did it just for the sake of doing something I never dreamed I could do.

One thing I'd never dreamed was how much fun it would turn out to be. All the times that I hung back afraid of being noticed in school, at parties, everywhere, I never imagined I could enjoy being the center of attention. Mama says you don't miss what you don't know. I guess she's right, but once you do know . . .

I could hardly believe what I was thinking. It wasn't like me. I don't go in for scheming and plotting. So why did I keep thinking that Sister Josephine had ordered me to stop with the petition *on school time* and *on school grounds*?

The way it turned out, I didn't need to take the petition around school anymore because I already had my signatures. True, I couldn't put the signed petitions in the principal's mailbox like Valerie and I had planned. Sister Josephine's order meant the principal's office was off-limits because it was on school grounds. But the city competition was being held miles away from the school. If I mailed the petition directly to the competition, dropping it in the mailbox near home after school closed, I wouldn't be doing anything Sister Josephine had forbidden.

It was such a clever idea that I giggled as I ran to my first class. Too bad I had to wait for school to finish so I could go over to Valerie's and tell her what I was going to do. On second thought, I decided to mail the petition first and then tell Valerie. After all, it was my petition.

18

Valerie

——

*A*ll my careful planning for going back to school paid off. Mrs. Go came early Monday morning to help me shower and dress. I examined my new outfit critically in the mirror. I couldn't see a trace of the leg brace, which was one worry off my mind.

My car came on time, and I spotted it immediately. Two problems accounted for.

First stop was the school office. The secretary took me right away (crutches get you fast service), said my forms were in order, and let me go to class. I soon realized I wasn't as far behind in my work as I'd feared. Actually, I'd kept up pretty well. That was a major problem out of the way.

I made it from room to room without bumping into anyone, getting caught in the elevator door, or slipping. So check off another set of worries.

I even lived through what I'd agonized over most: the reactions of the kids I knew before my accident. They either said, "How you doin'?" as if I hadn't changed since they saw me yesterday, or they said, "Welcome back," and pretended my crutches didn't matter. Either way, they didn't know what else to say, so they pretty much left me alone except for holding doors open for me.

Everything went as I'd planned. It all went better than I'd hoped. So why did I feel so down?

I told myself I was just tired. The school halls were longer and more crowded than I remembered, and my backpack got heavier and heavier as the day wore on. The classes were longer too, and there were more of them. By the time the car picked me up at three o'clock, I was so exhausted that even my good leg was shaky. It was a relief to sink into the backseat, close my eyes, and nap through the drive home.

Not home. The car pulled up in front of the center. It was like running the marathon, crossing the finish line, and then discovering they'd added another ten miles to the course. I was so tired I stumbled entering the lobby.

The guard steadied me. "Good to see you out of the wheelchair. Only you gotta be careful you don't overdo it."

I'd already overdone it; my legs were threatening to collapse under me. I was glad when the guard walked along with me as if he were going to P.T. too.

I lay on the padded table trying to bend and straighten my right knee. Rob measured how much I flexed it. "A little better than last week."

I couldn't stop myself asking the question I always asked when there was the tiniest bit of improvement. "Do you think the leg will ever get completely better?"

Rob gave me his usual answer. "Nobody knows. We

130

can only wait, work, and hope. Although we might know more if you let us do the tests again."

I shook my head at the mention of the tests. Then I asked, "My other leg is all right, isn't it?"

That wasn't my usual question. Rob wanted to know why I'd asked. Was I having a problem?

"No problem. My good leg is just a little shaky because it was my first day at school, and I was on it so much." But I was trembling all over.

He had me lift the leg, bend it, and kick it. He probed the muscles with his fingertips. "Does that hurt?"

I nodded dumbly. I was so terrified he'd find something terribly wrong that I didn't trust myself to speak. Waiting for the verdict, I broke into a sweat—the cold sweat of panic. I couldn't bear to become like Derek with both legs paralyzed. Or, worse still, like Lulu.

"It's only muscle fatigue from unaccustomed exercise."

"That's what I told you." If my leg was just tired, why did it feel so *weak*?

"How did school go?"

Remembering that Rob was responsible for my having to go back to school, and in case he still harbored the psychiatrist idea, I told him, "No sweat."

I told Mrs. Go the same thing when she met my car in front of the house.

By the time Amanda came home, I'd run out of strength to pretend. I told her, "I managed, but I'm exhausted."

"The first day is always the hardest." She patted my shoulder and I almost told her about the weakness in my good leg. But Rob had definitely said it was simple muscle strain, and it didn't make sense to worry her. There was absolutely no logical reason for either of us to worry about it. So why did I feel as if the ground was shaking under my feet, warning that an earthquake was about to crack the world open and drop me into a bottomless pit?

I said, "Teri's coming over. I think I'll do some writing in the meantime. I have an idea for a story about a woman who faces a firing squad and is pardoned at the last second. Did you know it actually happened to Dostoyevski?"

"I see you learned something interesting in school today."

"Actually, classes weren't the hard part . . ." I left the sentence dangling like a worm on a fishhook. If Amanda took the bait and asked what the hard part was, I might just possibly tell her. No, not possibly. Definitely. I took a deep breath and made up my mind: If she asked, I would definitely tell her.

She didn't ask. She patted my shoulder again and took out the work she'd brought home from the office. I opened my story journal.

The story didn't go well. I had no trouble imagining the execution. When I closed my eyes, I could feel the rough blindfold across my eyelids and the cold stone wall against my back. I could hear the metallic sounds of the soldiers loading their rifles. I tensed my body against the slam of bullets carrying eternal darkness. But that was as far as I got with the story. I could imagine dying. What I couldn't imagine was having my life given back to me. I was glad when Teri came and interrupted me.

Teri couldn't wait to get me alone in my room. "I have something important to tell you, but you have to promise not to breathe a word to a soul. I never told Mama or Rosanne about Sister Josephine calling me to her office, so don't say anything to them. Or to Marc, either."

I swore eternal silence before she could list each of the 230 million citizens of the United States individually.

Teri described the agony of waiting for Sister Josephine, how the idea of getting around Sister Josephine's edict dawned on her, and the clever way she wangled the city contest address from Peter. When she got to dropping the petition in the mailbox, I applauded.

She blushed as if no one had ever praised her before. "It's not such a big deal. I mean, I was real scared the whole time and I almost didn't go through with it at the last minute. Then I thought of what you said to me about if you could face the kids at school . . . So how was school?"

I said at least my used-to-be friends didn't stare or ask stupid questions. They just faded out of the picture because they didn't know how to treat me. She was indignant. "They're supposed to be so smart. Why didn't they treat you like they always do? You're still the same person you were before you hurt your leg. You're still you."

Good old Teri. It was exactly the right thing to say. The trouble is, it wasn't true. The familiar school routines pointed up that I wasn't me anymore. The old Valerie sprinted to classes after spending most of passing time discussing literature with good-looking guys. Now I trundled through the halls by my lonesome. People who used to run to catch up with me no longer noticed me. Because I wasn't a person anymore; I was a crippled thing on crutches. In spite of all my scheming to fit in, everyone else moved in a different world—a world where the light was brighter, the bells rang louder, the chalk dust was more pungent. A world that was closed to me forever.

Maybe if I'd tried to tell Teri how I felt, maybe if I'd

bared my soul to my friend, what happened later could have been avoided. But, although I felt the despair creeping up on me like a mugger on a dark street, the habit of keeping my pain to myself was too strong. Besides, Teri was part of the normal world. How could she understand?

I turned the conversation back to her. "Did you tell Peter about sending your petition to the city?"

"No. I didn't want to take the chance of Sister Josephine blaming him. It's enough that he signed the petition as president of the science club."

Although the windows were shut tight and the radiator was hissing heat, a cold wind from nowhere blew down my back. I shivered. The despair was closing in, and I was afraid it would never turn me loose again if I let it get a grip on me. I forced myself to smile and say, "Peter likes you."

"You mean as a girl? I know I'm too shy for most boys to notice, but Peter's shy too. He needs someone to listen when he decides to talk. And I really like listening to him."

Teri went on about how interesting and talented Peter was. I tried to listen because I really hoped it would work out for her. But I could hardly hear what she was saying. Although she was sitting barely three feet away, I had the strange sensation of her voice reaching me faintly through a long, dark tunnel. I wanted to cry, "Teri, come back." I picked up my crutches with some vague idea of trying to reach her.

"Valerie, where are you going?"

"Going? Oh. There's an article in the Sunday *Times* on artificial intelligence. I want to get it for Peter."

"But you're not wearing your brace. It's on the bed."

The despair was chasing me, and I had to outdistance it. "Rob's teaching me to walk short distances on crutches without it. The good leg does all the work."

I placed my crutches in position and stepped forward with my good leg exactly as Rob taught me. I shifted my weight onto the leg. It trembled and then gave way. I plopped back into the wheelchair.

As though nothing had happened, Teri asked, "Where's the article? I'll get it."

I whispered, "My good leg won't hold me."

"What?"

"The bloody leg collapsed."

"Are you sure? I thought you just decided to sit down."

I couldn't believe she was arguing with me. "It's my leg. I should know whether it's working or not."

"I better get your mother."

"No! Rob said it's only muscle strain."

"But if it's getting worse . . ."

We used to have a glass-topped coffee table in the living room until Dad dropped an ashtray on it and the glass shattered to pieces. The ashtray didn't hit very hard. It was the way it hit that did it. I was as brittle as glass. A tiny tap in the wrong place and I would shatter. I yelled, "Don't bug me!"

Teri just looked at me.

My phone rang. I gestured for her to answer it. When she hesitated, I gave her a fierce look. She lifted the receiver. "Hello. . . . Marc. . . . Of course I recognized your voice. . . . Yes, I came over to see Valerie."

I shook my head violently.

"She's fine. I mean, she's kind of tired because today was her first day back at school. . . . Oh, that's why you called."

I shook my head again.

"She's not here right now. . . . Where did she go? To play gin rummy with Mrs. Go. . . . No, I'm headed there now. . . . Yes, I'll tell Valerie you called. . . . Bye."

When Teri hung up, she looked at me accusingly. "Why did you make me lie to Marc? You're having one of those attacks you told me about, aren't you?"

"Don't be ridiculous."

"You are. I know you are." And she started to cry.

Doesn't that take the bloody cake? I was losing the use of my good leg, and *she* was crying.

She begged through her tears, "Valerie, please let me tell your mother or Rob or somebody who can help you."

"Remember that you swore on your baby brother's life to keep your mouth shut." I'd have told her it helped to have her care so much, but I was afraid of bringing on a fresh flood of tears. Another minute of her crying and she'd make me start, and once I started crying I'd dissolve completely and that would be the end of me. I held out a tissue. "Here, blow your nose. Stop making it into a federal case. I'll be okay. Now tell me what cute things Little Tony did today."

"Valerie, please."

"Tell me about the baby!"

"Well, I was dressing him in that little sweatshirt you bought him. I think what you wrote on it made Mama remember he has two sisters; she's letting me take care of him more. Anyway, just as I got it over his head . . ."

19

Teri

—❦—

osanne and I were cleaning our room Saturday. Vacuuming around my feet while I changed the bed, she commented, "That blanket is too loose."

"I like it that way."

She turned off the vacuum. "You're so edgy lately. Nobody can say a word to you without getting a fresh answer."

I guess I was on edge. Ever since I mailed off the petition, I kept expecting some terrible punishment for my sin. (The strange thing is, even though I was scared to death about what I'd done, I wasn't sorry I did it.) And I was worried about Valerie. Still, why was it okay for Rosanne to criticize my bed making and fresh for me to answer back? I said, "I have things on my mind."

She forgave me. "Want to tell me about it?"

I hesitated. Maybe Rosanne could help. "Say somebody told you something about herself. Like one of the girls at school. And you swore not to tell a soul. But that person was in trouble, and it might help her if you revealed her secret. What would you do?"

"Who is it? Julia?"

"Rosanne!"

"Okay. The answer is simple. You try to convince her to tell her parents or her priest or her doctor. You try very hard. Then, if she won't listen, you have to do it for her. For her own good."

It sounded right. But I remembered how mad Valerie gets about people interfering in other people's lives.

I went into the kitchen where Mama was feeding Little Tony. He opened his mouth wide for the spoon, like a baby bird. I made a smiley face at him. He smiled back, and mashed banana oozed out of his mouth. Mama handed me the spoon. While I scooped the goo off the baby's chin and back into his mouth, I asked her, "Say a girl you knew told you . . ."

Unlike Rosanne, Mama didn't think it was so simple. "Are you sure it will help this girl if you tell her secret?"

That was the trouble: I wasn't sure. I wasn't even sure that I wasn't making a big deal out of nothing. You know how it is when you start worrying; sometimes you get carried away. I mean, I'd be miserable too if I had an accident, and when I went back to school, my old friends treated me like a freak.

The doorbell rang. Mama said, "That's Marco with the oranges. Aunt Flo's friend sent her a whole crate from Florida, so she's giving us some."

I couldn't let Marc see me looking like an unmade bed. I ran to the bathroom. When I came back washed and combed, Marc was sitting in the living room. He asked how my petition was going. I said, "Okay" and changed the subject, "It was funny my answering Valerie's phone when you called the other night."

He laughed. "Don't ever play poker. People can spot you bluffing from up in the Bronx."

"It wasn't like what you're thinking. Valerie was exhausted from school and the center, and besides her leg was bothering her. Both her legs, so . . ."

"Whoa. She called me last night and explained. Poor kid, she has to go for those tests next week."

"Tests? She didn't say anything about tests when I spoke to her on . . ." Monday. Because I'd been afraid Valerie would read my mind and know I was thinking about telling on her, I'd taken the coward's way out. I hadn't called since I saw her last Monday.

I ran to the phone. Valerie said actually she hadn't noticed my not calling because she was busy catching up with school. She said naturally she called Marc back. She wasn't letting a gorgeous fish like that off her hook even if she didn't want to reel him in. When I asked about the tests, she said they were no big deal. Rob had nagged her to have them for ages, but she'd stalled because of the needles. Now she'd decided there were worse things than being a pin cushion. She sounded so together that I felt stupid for worrying. Thank goodness I hadn't told Rosanne who I was worrying about.

Valerie said if Marc and I had nothing better to do, why didn't we come over and keep her company because Amanda had to see a client and Mrs. Go was visiting her son.

When we got there, Valerie entertained us with funny stories about this birdbrain who runs the elevator at her school. It seems the kids pull all kinds of far-out stunts to con him into letting them ride without a pass, and he falls for every one. You wouldn't believe the tricks they pull. Valerie reported them deadpan. Marc and I were in stitches.

Then she did a description of the tests she was having next Tuesday. She made it sound like a comedy/horror film with mad scientists shooting electric sparks through this crazy machine at her. Not to be a party pooper, I tried to smile. But I didn't think it was funny. The tests sounded horrible. Just thinking about them made my skin crawl. I couldn't help asking, "Aren't you a little nervous about the needles?"

"Don't be a nerd." But she got suddenly quiet. It was like somebody'd turned off the TV.

Without her funny stories, there didn't seem much to say. To make conversation, I asked Marc, "Did Aunt Flo see the tree lighting yesterday?" and explained to Valerie, "She goes to Rockefeller Plaza every year to watch them light the big Christmas tree."

Marc nodded. "She said it was the most beautiful tree ever."

"She always says that." Which took care of that subject.

Marc doesn't have patience to sit around doing nothing. He likes action. "I have an idea. I'll take you girls to see the tree."

I asked, "Now?" and Marc said, "Sure," and I said, "Let's see the store windows too. Lord and Taylor is always great."

Valerie said, "Some other time."

I asked why not now, and Valerie said parking there was impossible, and Marc said he knew a guy who ran a garage on Forty-seventh Street. Valerie said she'd get knocked over in the crowd, and Marc said he'd protect her, and I said let's go, and Valerie said maybe next week. It went on like that till Valerie shouted, "I don't want to see the effing tree!"

Marc said, "Temper, temper."

Valerie said, "I'm getting a Coke," and wheeled herself out of the room without asking if we wanted any.

I whispered to Marc, "There was no reason for her to blow up like that."

"Valerie's a girl who always wants to have her own way."

"I guess so. But doesn't she seem awfully . . . moody? She goes up and down like an elevator. I mean, she was so cheerful when we first came. Then she got all quiet. Then she was suddenly angry."

When Marc shook his head like he didn't know what I was talking about, I said, "Maybe I'm imagining things." Maybe I was. Marc didn't see anything wrong. But I couldn't make myself believe it was all my imagination.

Valerie was balancing three cans of soda on her wheelchair arm as she maneuvered the chair back through the doorway. She offered two cans to Marc and me, acting so friendly that it was hard to believe she'd practically bitten our heads off before she went for them.

As I opened mine, it suddenly occurred to me that Valerie had been in her wheelchair the whole time we were here. She often sits in it because regular chairs make her back hurt, but she usually uses crutches to go to another room because the wheelchair is a tight fit through doors. Today she hadn't left the wheelchair once. I asked, "How come you're not using your crutches today?"

She smiled serenely at Marc. "Will you please explain to Ms. Worrywart over there that my legs are tired from a week of school and I'm resting them."

Remembering her collapsing back into her chair the last time I saw her, I blurted out, "There's nothing wrong with your good leg, is there?" Then I could've bitten my tongue off. How could I put such an idea into her head? Now she'd really be upset. And with good reason.

Strangely, it didn't seem to bother her. She shrugged. "They're doing tests to be sure."

Testing her *good* leg! I couldn't help thinking about the story she wrote about this girl who got paralyzed bit by bit till she could only control her eyelids. I wanted to run over and hug Valerie and promise her everything was going to be fine. But she acted like she didn't have a care in the world. She started telling Marc about some Russian writer and a firing squad. So I just sat there.

I sat and worried if maybe Rosanne was right. Maybe I should tell someone or do something. But who? What?

20

Valerie

———

I was as calm as the eye of a hurricane. (That's a nice image. I must save it for a story.) The doctor dabbed goo on my ankle and fastened on a gizmo attached to a computer by a wire. He explained, "When current flows through the electrode, the computer shows how much electricity it takes to make each muscle move. I'll start low and gradually increase it."

I said, "I know the drill. I had it done in the hospital."

"Then we'll start."

Amanda took my hand. "If it gets too bad at any point, the doctor can stop." Her hand was cold in mine. She was more nervous than I was. Actually, I wasn't nervous at all. I already knew what the test would show.

The computer clicked. The doctor asked, "Do you feel this?"

"No."

"This?"

"I think so."

He attached another electrode. Or maybe he moved the same one. I was staring at the wavy lines wiggling across the computer screen.

"Do you feel this?"

"No."

"This?"

"A little."

It went on and on. I'd forgotten how long it takes. I wished he'd get it over with and give me the bad news. Then the computer chattered like an angry monkey, and lightning struck me. I screamed.

Amanda asked the doctor was that necessary, and he said he hadn't realized the left leg was normal because the referral form said suspected nerve damage. Amanda patted my hand and said that was wonderful news and try to hang on.

The next shocks weren't as bad, but they were bad enough. By the time he took the last electrode off, my jaw ached from gritting my teeth. Then came the needles. I don't want to talk about the needles. I want to forget them.

Finally, it was over. The doctor said I was a good patient. He said that my left leg was normal and there was some improvement in my right leg.

Amanda insisted on stopping in the coffee shop on the way out. She said she'd been too nervous to eat breakfast. Now she wanted to celebrate with a piece of pie. Cherry pie. Cherry pie à la mode.

As I sat stirring a Coke with a straw, a familiar voice asked, "How were the tests?"

144

I looked up. "I haven't had such a stupendous time since Gran took me to the Royal Shakespeare Theatre in London."

Amanda said, "You must be Rob. I recognized your voice from the phone. The tests were difficult for Valerie, but the results are encouraging." Then she repeated what the doctor had told her.

Rob frowned. "You're sure the left leg is normal?"

Amanda is a successful businesswoman. It annoys her when men question her accuracy. "Of course I'm sure. Speak to the doctor yourself if you doubt my word."

"I'm not doubting you. I'm puzzled that the tests don't explain the symptoms Valerie is experiencing."

Amanda pushed the rest of her pie away. "Please sit down. I'd appreciate hearing more about Valerie's symptoms. She told me you diagnosed muscle strain."

"That's what I thought at first. However, Valerie's leg seems to be growing weaker. Yesterday it wouldn't support her weight."

I said, "I only weigh a hundred and twelve."

Amanda gave me a strange look. Then she turned to Rob. "Do you have any idea what is causing the weakness?"

"The tests may still tell us. The doctor only gave you his first impressions. When he analyzes the data, he'll have a complete picture."

I said, "He can analyze until he turns pea green. It won't keep my good leg from becoming paralyzed too."

"Val, you mustn't say that!" Amanda was upset enough to raise her voice so that a woman in the next booth stared. She continued more softly, "Should the tests finally show anything, it has to be slight or the doctor would have seen it at first glance. So there is absolutely no reason for your fears."

I wasn't afraid. I just knew what was happening to me. The advantage to knowing the worst is that there is nothing to be afraid of anymore.

21

Teri

———

*H*istory was my last class. I pulled my mind away from Valerie having her tests this morning and concentrated on copying the dates the teacher was putting on the board. Since I sent in the petition, I'd worked my head off in school. Like being good would save me from Sister Josephine.

Shortly before the final bell, a monitor came in with a note. The teacher read it and said, "Teresa, Sister Josephine wants you."

I'd told myself over and over that Sister Josephine was going to eat me alive—like scaring myself would keep it from happening. It was happening anyway. I stuttered, "N-now?"

"Now. Take your things with you."

On the way to Sister Josephine's office, I remembered Valerie's story about this Russian writer who got dragged in front of a firing squad. I knew just how he felt.

Sister Josephine kept me standing and waiting while

she finished writing something. Probably a note to my parents. Suicide is a sin, but I wished I was dead.

Finally, she fixed her eyes on me. "I had a telephone call from Dr. Meeks at the city science competition. He informed me that you submitted a petition to him. A petition containing two hundred and six signatures."

Two hundred and six! I was in such a rush to mail the petition that I didn't count them. I never dreamed there were so many. "I got all the signatures before you told me to stop, and I mailed the petition at home after school hours."

"You appear to have a talent for finding loopholes in the law."

I hung my head in shame.

She let me suffer before she told me, "Dr. Meeks decided that since you received first honorable mention, I may submit your project with the other prize winners—if I wish."

Hope fluttered in my heart. And died again. After what I did, why should she want to? I prayed fervently to St. Jude, patron of desperate cases.

"Since Dr. Meeks will permit it, I see no reason why there should not be six chances to bring honor to our school instead of five."

It was like a heavenly choir suddenly burst into a chorus of hallelujahs. I gasped, "Oh, thank you. Thank you."

"I want it understood that this is not an endorsement of the methods you used to bring your project to the attention of the city committee. Although some people might admire your initiative." And she smiled. The corners of her mouth only curled up a fraction of an inch, but it was definitely a smile. I stared in amazement.

Then her lips pursed into their usual stern expression. "You may go."

I walked out of the building in a daze. I still couldn't believe it. I, Teri D'Angelo, the good girl who always did what she was told, had defied Sister Josephine. And I won!

Julia was waiting outside to find out what happened.

I told her, "Sister Josephine's sending my solar house to the city contest with the other prizewinners."

Julia yelled the news to Patsy. In a minute, I was surrounded by people congratulating me and telling me how glad they were they'd signed my petition.

It was wonderful. I lapped up the congratulations like a cat with a big dish of milk. I'd never felt so strong and smart in my life. Even though a cold raw wind was threatening snow, I felt toasty warm inside.

After a while, everyone else got cold. Saying they were rooting for me to win a scholarship, they headed home. I took the bus straight to Valerie's house. The petition was originally her idea. I wanted to share my happiness with her.

Valerie said she wished she'd seen Sister Josephine's face. She said I might even win a scholarship; stranger things had happened. She said all the right things. But her heart didn't seem in it.

It made me uneasy. The thing about Valerie is that she never does things halfway. She curses the worst, tells the most fascinating stories, acts the brattiest, and comes up with ideas I'd never dream of in a million years. She's the most interesting, maddening, wonderful friend a girl ever had. Now she seemed flat and dull.

But how could I expect her to get excited about my

news with what she had on her mind? Feeling guilty for not doing it earlier, I asked, "How were the tests?"

"I survived."

"At least it's over. When do you get the results?"

She recited like she was reading the doctor's report, "There is some improvement in the right leg. The left leg is normal."

"That's wonderful! I didn't want to say anything, but I was scared there was really something wrong with your good leg. Boy, am I relieved. It's a great day for both of us."

Valerie looked at me like I was one of those insensitive clods who are always trying to cheer her up. I defended myself. "I know your right leg still isn't well. But if the tests show it's improving . . ."

"Eff the tests." She picked up a book and pretended to read. Or maybe she really was reading. I wouldn't put it past her. She turned a page.

Exasperated, I demanded, "Am I supposed to sit here while you read that whole damn book?"

She looked up, "Damn? I never heard you use a 'bad word' before."

"Dammit. If something's bothering you, talk about it. Or don't. But don't play some kind of game I don't understand."

Valerie's smile reminded me of Sister Josephine's when she said some people might admire my initiative. She said, "The needles affected my good leg. I can't move it anymore."

I was stunned. I thought she was having a despair attack, and I was going to threaten to tell somebody if she didn't do it herself. But a paralyzed leg is different. It isn't in your mind. It's real. I was scared, and I didn't know what

150

to do. I asked stupidly, "What did the doctor say when you couldn't move your good leg?"

"The leg only got so bad after I came home."

"Didn't your mother call him?"

"She went back to work as soon as she brought me home."

How could Valerie be so calm? *Both* her legs were paralyzed, and she was acting like she got spaghetti sauce on her sweater—a shame, but it would wash out. I tried to sound calm too. "We should call your mother right away."

"Why? The leg'll still be the same when she gets home."

I saw a ray of hope. "Maybe it won't. Maybe it's just temporary. From the shocks and needles and things."

Valerie shook her head. "The leg was failing before. The tests just finished it off. It would've happened soon anyway."

"You can't be sure of that."

She didn't bother to answer. She didn't seem to care. She opened her book again. I watched her eyes moving. She really was reading. I shouted, "Put that down and talk to me!"

Holding her place with her finger, she asked, "What do you want to talk about?"

I felt so confused and helpless. There was a wall around her that I couldn't get through. "I'm calling your mother. Maybe if she talks to the doctor, he'll say this happens all the time from the tests and you'll be fine tomorrow."

"I wouldn't bet on it."

I went to the kitchen phone where Amanda's number was posted in case of emergency. This was an emergency. So why did I feel like I was doing something awful to Valerie?

I took a deep breath and dialed.

22

Valerie

---

*I*t snowed. Then it turned bitterly cold, and the snow froze solid. It was too slippery for me to go to school or to the center. I sat in my wheelchair and did jigsaw puzzles. I liked the way the puzzle pieces fit together so neatly. Even odd-shaped pieces that looked like they couldn't possibly fit anywhere eventually dropped into place. Dad sent me three new puzzles. I finished them in three days.

When the streets were clear again, Amanda made an appointment with a new specialist to retest my legs. I let her take me. I let him examine me. When he got to the needles, I discovered I'd become less sensitive to pain.

Amanda told me, "The tests show that your left leg is completely normal."

"The tests are wrong."

I went back to the center. Rob said, "Try to lift your left knee."

"I'm trying. Nothing happens."

Dad came to see me. He said, "I know you can do it."

"I can't."

Gran called from England, "What can I do to help?"

"There's nothing anyone can do."

Rob decided I should see the center psychiatrist. Amanda begged me to cooperate. She was taking it so hard that I agreed to go. Anyway, what did it matter?

The center psychiatrist wasn't an idiot like the hospital guy. She was a pleasant young woman with carroty hair and freckles. Her friends probably call her Red. When she asked what was bothering me, I told her, "Actually, I'm adjusting well. In my psychology class, the teacher defined a healthy adjustment to life as changing what can be changed and accepting what can't be changed."

She said she agreed. "But the problem is deciding what can be changed and what can't."

"I can't change the fact that my legs are paralyzed."

"Do you wonder why it took so long for the paralysis to show up in the second leg?"

I shrugged. I was losing interest. Actually, I wasn't interested to start with. I'd get Amanda to buy me a new puzzle later.

"Does it bother you?"

"Does what bother me?" A thousand-piece puzzle.

"Are you unhappy about losing the use of your legs?"

"Of course I am." I swung one of my dangling earrings absently back and forth with my finger. They were the ones Teri gave me for my birthday.

"You seem quite calm about it."

"Making a fuss won't bring my legs back." I swung the other earring. Teri'd invited me to Christmas Eve dinner. Her family began the holiday celebration on Christmas

Eve with an elaborate seafood meal. I said I'd go if I wasn't too tired. The less I do, the more tired I become.

The psychiatrist opened a folder. "You didn't used to be calm. Your occupational therapist calls you 'disruptive.' "

Why should I care what smarmy old Eunice wrote? Why should I care about anything?

She flipped a page. "Rob, on the other hand, says you are intelligent, creative, and hardworking when you are motivated. He also says you never let anyone know that you hurt."

Wishing she'd shut up, I reached for the earring again. My hand trembled. Just a little. But I stopped breathing. The air in the room seemed to have gotten thick and syrupy. I was having trouble drawing it into my lungs.

I closed my hand into a tight fist to stop the shaking. Slowly, with great care, I lowered my arm until my fist was resting on my knee. I opened my hand and stared at my fingers. They were trembling.

Then I knew. My hand was going too. The paralysis was creeping up my body. The story I wrote was coming true. Soon there would be nothing left of me but my brain.

The psychiatrist was asking me something. I could see her lips moving, but the thick air kept her voice from reaching me.

The air shimmered like dirty-gray Jell-o. Then the gray turned to black. For the first time in my life, I fainted.

23

Teri

———

I bought Little Tony a plastic ball with chimes inside for Christmas. He laughed when I rolled the ball at him and it played "Jingle Bells." Rosanne said he was at the stage where he laughs at everything. I said he was laughing because he liked his new toy, and she answered that he probably did like it. She was going out of her way to be kind to me. The way she was so careful of my feelings, you'd think I was the one who'd had the breakdown instead of Valerie.

Ever since I met Valerie, I wanted to be like her. I wanted to have the nerve to do what *I* wanted whether other people liked it or not. So I watched Valerie, and I learned. I learned enough to stand up to Sister Josephine. Now Valerie had cracked up and was in a sanatorium. No, not a sanatorium. She hates euphem . . . pretty words for unpleasant things. She was in a mental hospital. An insane asylum, booby hatch, funny farm, nuthouse. If Valerie—who I thought had all the answers—could lose her mind as easy as dropping an earring stud down the shower drain, where did that leave me?

I'd been worried about her, but I never expected anything like this. I was calling her every day and she was all right. Kind of down, but who wouldn't be down if her good leg didn't work and the doctors did awful tests and still couldn't find out what was wrong? Valerie said the tests didn't bother her, but she always liked to act like nothing got to her.

Then, without any warning, one evening I called and her mother told me that Valerie was in this sanatorium. She said Valerie was suffering from depression and something called "conversion hysteria." I knew what depression was—feeling miserable—but I was too shook up to ask what the other thing meant. I guess I didn't really want to know.

It wasn't till I had this nightmare that I asked Rosanne to look it up in her nursing books. In my nightmare, Valerie was locked in a dark cell with water dripping down the stone walls and rats running across her bare feet. She was shaking the bars and screaming for me to get her out.

Rosanne's book said: "Paralysis or weakness which has no physical cause but is an expression of a mental state." Rosanne explained, "It means when something so painful happens to a person that she shuts it out of her mind, it makes her body sick instead. Probably in Valerie's case it was her accident. A person like her who needs to be the best at everything has a terrible time adjusting to being disabled."

"But why did they put her in a sanatorium? Valerie's not crazy. She didn't do anything weird or hurt anybody. It's not fair for them to lock her up. I dreamed about that place. It was like a dungeon in some old castle." I shuddered and my eyes filled with tears. "It's so awful for her to be there."

"It's not like in your dream. Sweetwater is a rich people's sanatorium. I had a patient who was there for her drinking, and she said it's practically like a hotel. You'll see when you visit."

I blew my nose. "Valerie's mother didn't say I could visit." The thought of going into that place made me sick to my stomach.

"Of course you can. I'll check the hours for you."

Rosanne came back with the hours and travel directions neatly written down. As I shoved the paper into my pocket, she said, "You're nervous about going, aren't you? I'd go with you except I have finals coming up."

"That's okay. I'm fine."

"No, you're not. You're scared stiff."

How did I ever imagine I could be strong and brave like Valerie? Nobody could talk Valerie out of visiting her friend Lulu in the hospital. She went on crutches. But now that Valerie was in a sanatorium, I was praying for a blizzard or transit strike to keep me away. Knowing that my conscience would make me go anyway—even if I had to walk the whole way through ten feet of snow—didn't stop me feeling like a coward.

Rosanne said, "Let's ask Marc to drive you. I'm sure Valerie'd love to see him too."

I shook my head no, but it's hard to stop Rosanne.

There was a brick wall around Sweetwater. At least it wasn't topped with barbed wire or broken glass. But Marc and I ran out of things to say as we drove up to the gate.

We'd been talking the whole drive up. I told him the city scholarships would be awarded after the Christmas vacation and he told me stories about the funny people he meets being a salesman. Like if we kept talking about other things we wouldn't have to think about where we were going and why.

I got butterflies in my stomach when the guard stopped us at the gate. Even though he just asked who we were visiting and told us where to park, the butterflies wouldn't settle down.

They got worse when we left the safety of the car, crossed the snowy grounds, and went through a big carved door into the building. Rosanne said Sweetwater was once some millionaire's estate. She said to look around and tell her what it was like, because a nurse needs information about different facilities. I was too busy trying not to throw up to look.

Valerie was in the recreation room. Her wheelchair was pulled up to a table with a jigsaw puzzle on it, and she was staring down at the puzzle. She was wearing her Jane Austen sweatshirt and jeans. At least she wasn't in a hospital robe. But she was sitting so still it made me nervous. She reminded me of those marble tomb statues you see at the Cloisters.

I put a smile on my face and walked over. "Hi, Valerie. That looks like a hard puzzle."

"Don't touch." Her hand shot out, grabbed a purple piece, and dropped it into a hole. "There, that completes the wall."

I tried not to feel hurt. I told myself she was absorbed in her puzzle. She got that way sometimes. She used to say she had "phenomenal powers of concentration."

Marc put down the cake box we'd brought and told Valerie I made him drive down to Mulberry Street to buy cannoli like the only bakery in the world was in Little Italy. Valerie said, "Thanks," but she kept her eyes glued to the puzzle. She fitted in two blue pieces and reached for a brown one.

The brown piece didn't fit. When she tried to jam it in, it got stuck halfway. Annoyed, she pushed herself away from the table.

You'd think that once she gave up on the puzzle she'd say "Glad to see you" or something. She didn't. She just stared out the window like we weren't there. There was a long awkward silence. As the visitors, I guess it was up to us to make conversation, but I couldn't think of anything to say. I looked to Marc, who was born with the gift of gab. He seemed to be struck dumb.

Finally I managed, "Rosanne told me this house used to belong to a millionaire. How about showing us around?"

She shook her head. Not even a shake, more a twitch.

Thank goodness Marc came to life and started to coax her. And lucky no girl can resist Marc's coaxing. Otherwise we would've stood there like statues for the next hour.

Valerie gave us the tour. She rattled off information like a tour guide who's said the same thing a thousand times before. She told us the rec room used to be the millionaire's ballroom. In the dining room, she pointed out the fireplace he got from some palace in Europe. I tried to pay attention for Rosanne, but my eyes kept sneaking to Valerie's legs, which were propped on the wheelchair footrests like two pieces of wood. Valerie didn't notice that I wasn't listening to her spiel. I don't think she was listening, either.

When we got back to the rec room, she stopped talking like someone had turned off the tape. She picked up a puzzle piece, tried it in a couple of places, and dropped it back in the box. Marc and I watched her. Finally he asked, "Want a cannoli?"

Valerie muttered she wasn't hungry.

Marc said he was, and he broke the string around the box. He and I split a cannoli. Valerie didn't even take a taste. I felt stupid for running all over town to buy them. Stupid for coming in the first place.

Then I told myself I had to make allowances. With all its fancy fireplaces and things, this was no hotel. It was a sanatorium and Valerie was . . . sick. So why did I have the feeling she was being difficult on purpose?

Pushing the feeling down, I started chattering about how cute Little Tony was. "He laughs at everything now. You have to come see him."

She gave me a ghost of the old green-eyed Valerie stare.

"I mean, when your leg gets better."

Another stare.

"How is your leg? What do the doctors say?"

She smiled. A strange little smile. "Don't you know? It's all in my head. That's why I'm here."

That night I had the dream again. Valerie was in the same dark cell. Only this time she wasn't shaking the bars. She was sitting on the filthy floor fitting broken pieces of glass together. The glass was sharp and her fingers were bleeding. Marc said, "You should do something." I asked, "Why me?" He said, "Because she's your friend."

160

24

Valerie

———

ctually, Sweetwater wasn't bad once I got used to it. I didn't mind the food tasting like fried cardboard because I didn't have any appetite. And although the bed felt as if it were carved from a block of wood, I fell asleep the second my head hit the pillow and slept a solid ten hours a night. I woke in the mornings to a routine that carried me along without any effort on my part: breakfast, exercise, lunch, session with the psychiatrist (Monday, Wednesday, and Friday), free time (to do puzzles), dinner, TV, bed. No school, no center, no having to see anyone from the outside world except Saturday and Sunday afternoons. I told the psychiatrist (male this time), "It's like being back in the womb."

"Do you think your symptoms might be a way of hiding from things that are troubling you?"

When the psychiatrist talked about my symptoms, I had the feeling we were discussing a case history in a psych book. The sort of case that reads: "V.R. is a fifteen-year-old female in good health except for an accident that paralyzed her right leg. Some months after the accident, she began having fantasies of her entire body becoming paralyzed. Although all tests show her left leg to be completely normal, she is unable to move it." I forgot we were talking about me, and my mind wandered.

The pills they gave me made it easy not to pay attention. At first, they made me feel as if I were moving in slow motion. Actually, the floating feeling was rather pleasant. When it wore off after a week or so, I asked the psychiatrist to up the dosage. He acted as if I were a drug addict and cut the pills back instead. That didn't stop the days from drifting by like the clouds I watched through the rec room window.

I was always surprised when the weekend rolled around again and Amanda arrived with puzzles, magazines, books, cookies, my Walkman, my story journal. Anything and everything she could think of to tempt me back to the land of the living. She brought a biography of the Jersey Lily from Gran, a quilted robe from Dad, a potted plant from Mrs. Go, a poster from Derek and Fran. She brought swatches of material for me to choose new curtains for my bedroom. She promised to have the curtains up by the time I came home. Which, she said, was sure to be soon.

Teri came too. She brought pictures of Little Tony, homemade lasagna in a stay-hot bag from her mother, body lotion from Rosanne, and a get-well card signed by her whole family. She told me how much everybody missed me.

Amanda and Teri tried to tempt, bribe, and coax me into leaving the safety of Sweetwater for the treacherous world that had crippled my body and my soul. They tried so hard that I was sorry to disappoint them. But I couldn't help myself. I couldn't go back.

Actually, I didn't want to.

25

Teri

I tried everything I could think of to make Valerie feel
better. To make her stop acting so . . .

I can't quite describe how Valerie acted when I went
to visit her. I tried to explain it to Rosanne. "It's not like
Valerie to be so . . . good. I mean, she always thanks me
for the stuff I bring—even though she doesn't really look
at it. And when I talk to her, she answers like she swal-
lowed the Miss Manners book. Like when I was excited
over Peter winning a scholarship in the city competition,
she said, 'Congratulations' and wished me the same luck
next time. And when I told her the whole petition thing
really got me thinking about going to college, maybe even
engineering school like she suggested, she said that was
wise of me. Except I had the feeling she didn't really hear
what I was saying. Or what she was saying either. It's like
she isn't really *there*."

Rosanne said, "You don't understand mental illness."

I guess I didn't. I wanted to yell at Valerie to stop whatever she was doing.

Mama said, "It's hard to keep trying when it doesn't seem it's making any difference. But you're showing Valerie that you care about her, and that has to help."

"Do you really think so?"

She gave me a hug. "I know so."

So I went every Saturday afternoon religiously. I brought cute stuff—an *I'm the Best* button and a teeny notebook—and lugged the food Mama sent on the train and bus. I even got Papa to teach me to play gin rummy because I thought it might cheer Valerie up to beat me.

Valerie said "Gin" like she couldn't care less.

"Shoot! I just needed one more card. Now I'm stuck with two kings and a queen."

She started sorting puzzle pieces while I added up the score. She was always fiddling with a puzzle or staring out the window. It was like she was building an invisible wall around herself thicker and higher than the brick wall around Sweetwater. I reminded myself that Mama said my being there was helping Valerie, but it was so frustrating.

I announced, "Your game. I owe you eighty-three cents. Let's play again."

She turned her head toward the window. "No, thanks."

She could at least look at me! I put on a cheerful smile. "Have it your way, but I won't pay you now. I'll save the money to buy you an ice cream cone when you get home. They opened this store on Columbus Avenue where the ice cream is so chocolaty you think you died and went to heaven."

She didn't bother to answer.

I tried to have patience. But she made me so mad. It's funny: I don't remember ever getting mad before I knew Valerie. I mean, everyone gets angry sometimes. Mama and Papa fight about money and about Aunt Paula sticking her nose in where it doesn't belong. And Rosanne carried on for a week the time I borrowed her best blouse without asking and got black grease on it. But I never lost my temper. I just felt hurt. I remember once when Papa had a hard day at the garage and picked on Mama and Rosanne and the three of them were yelling fit to bust. I just stood there wondering what it felt like to be angry.

Now I knew. I mean, I give up my Saturdays to drag up here by bus and train and another bus, and what do I get for it? Puzzles and windows is what I get. Sure I was hurt, but I was mad too. I wanted to smack Valerie for the way she was treating me. And smack her harder for what she was doing to herself.

I lifted my hand—and looked at my watch. "I wonder what's keeping your mother." If that made Valerie think I was anxious to leave, she was too right. And if she thought I was coming back next week to sit and watch her stare out the window, forget it. The department stores were having good sales. I would call Julia and Patsy to go shopping with me next Saturday. They'd been my friends all my life. Why should I let those friendships slip through my fingers because we didn't live on the same block anymore? We could meet at Macy's. Like Rosanne always tells me: It just takes a little get up and go.

Valerie's mother hurried in. "Sorry I'm late, but I was on the phone with Gran. The new medicine helped so much that her doctor says if she's careful not to get over-tired, she can make the trip to New York. Gran will be here to see you next Saturday. Isn't that wonderful?"

Valerie said that was nice. You'd think she'd show a little enthusiasm. It was bad enough her acting like I was the postman delivering junk mail, but her grandmother is supposed to be Valerie's favorite person in the whole world. And she was coming all the way from England to visit.

I said I had to be going because it was a long ride back, and Papa liked me home before dark.

Valerie's mother said, "I know Valerie appreciates your coming all this way to visit her."

How could she tell? If Valerie appreciated anything, she sure had a strange way of showing it. But I nodded politely.

"At least I can offer you a ride next Saturday. The train is too tiring for my mother, so I'm arranging for a car. Do ride with us. That is, if you're planning to come."

What could I say? That I wasn't planning to come back next Saturday or ever? That I was tired of trying to be Mother Teresa? That when I did something for somebody, I expected her to notice or I'd go shopping instead?

I was ashamed to say any of those things. I was ashamed of even feeling them. Valerie was sick, and I couldn't abandon her. I said, "If it isn't out of your way . . ."

"We'll pick you up at noon. My mother will be pleased to meet Valerie's best friend."

Best friend. Now I really felt like a louse. I made a solemn vow to be more patient and understanding next week.

167

26

Valerie

——

Breakfast, exercise, lunch, psychiatrist, dinner, TV,
bed, breakfast, walk, lunch, puzzle, dinner, book,
bed, breakfast . . .

The days went round and round like the prayer wheels
the Tibetan monks spin. Around and around, repeating
endlessly. As the wheel spun, it got smaller—folding in
on itself like a dying star, shriveling like a dead worm in
the hot sun.

"What are you thinking about?" the psychiatrist asked
me. He was so eager that I was almost tempted to tell
him the prayer wheel fantasy so he'd have something to
write in his notebook.

The temptation passed. Nothing holds my interest for
long. Besides, I was afraid he'd interfere with the process.
I shrugged. The wheel spun on.

Then it stopped. It was Saturday, and Gran was coming.

Why did Gran have to come? I didn't want to see her. I didn't want to see anybody. Why didn't they all leave me alone? Why didn't they let me shrivel up and die in peace?

27

Teri

~

acy's was having this terrific sale on winter coats, practically giving them away, and my pea jacket looked like some sailor swabbed the decks with it. I needed a new coat desperately. I told myself that Valerie's mother and grandmother were both going to visit her today, so she didn't need me. I told myself Valerie wouldn't die if I missed one Saturday. But I couldn't convince myself.

I once asked Mama why she always goes running when somebody needs her, and she said, "How could I not go?" I'm Valerie's best friend—her mother said so—and I really want to help her. So how could I not go? I just wish Valerie'd let herself be helped. I wish she didn't make me feel like a selfish pig if I didn't visit her and like a doormat if I did.

Anyway, I was ashamed to call at the last minute to say I'd changed my mind. At least I didn't have to make the trip by train today. Even though I wasn't looking forward to the ride. Valerie's mother is nice to me, but somehow I always feel like I wore the wrong clothes or I'm talking too loud. It'd be worse with her grandmother in the car too.

Valerie's grandmother looked so royal that I almost curtsied like you're supposed to for the queen. And she talked in that high-class British accent from "Masterpiece Theater." But she acted like Aunt Flo. She asked where I got the red rose I was carrying, and I said my cousin Marc sent it. She wanted to know all about Marc, and in no time we were chatting like family. I told her Marc was a heartbreaker and she asked if he broke Valerie's heart, and I told her Valerie was the only girl I knew who didn't flip over him, and she said Valerie liked to be different, and I said Valerie wasn't as different as she made out, and she said I was a shrewd young lady. I liked her a lot. It was easy to see why Valerie loved her so much.

So why didn't Valerie show she loved her grandmother? I mean, she just said "Hi, Gran" like she saw her yesterday. If my grandmother came three thousand miles specially to see me, I'd throw my arms around her and hug and kiss her. I know Valerie doesn't come from a hugging family, but she should do *something*.

What she did was send me to find a vase for Marc's rose.

An aide gave me a vase meant for a big bouquet. The rose looked silly floating around in about a gallon of water, but Valerie said it was romantic. She stared at it, tilting her head to one side like a critic examining a statue or painting. I couldn't figure out why it fascinated her so. It's not like she's crazy about Marc or anything.

The way she kept looking at the silly flower instead of

talking to us began to get on my nerves. I hadn't given up shopping for a new coat today just to stand there like the Flowers by Wire delivery man.

I could see it bothered Gran too. She started telling Valerie about how she persuaded the doctor to let her come and how lovely the stewardesses were when she got a little dizzy on the plane.

Valerie just said, "Um" and "Really?"

I tried to make allowances for Valerie's being sick. But it was getting harder and harder. How could Valerie be too sick to see that Gran was dying to be told that Valerie was happy to see her? I prompted her, "Isn't it great that your grandmother could come?"

Valerie said, "Yes," but she kept staring at the rose. I know Rosanne says Valerie isn't responsible for her actions, but it looked to me like Valerie knew exactly what she was doing. It looked like she was deliberately ignoring us.

It really hurts me to give up my Saturday to visit Valerie and have her act like she's doing me a favor if she says "Hello." And I'm not an old woman with a heart condition who traveled all the way from England. I'm not family. How much worse it must be for Gran.

I started to get mad. Not for myself. For Gran. But I took a deep breath and reminded myself of my vow of patience and understanding. Patiently, I tried to show Valerie how she was supposed to act by telling Gran I was sure it made a big difference to Valerie to know her grandmother loved her enough to risk her own health to fly halfway across the world to spend a few hours with her and cheer her up.

Valerie didn't take the hint. She didn't say, "Yes, Gran,

it makes me feel better to have you here." Instead she started fiddling with a puzzle piece. First the rose, now the puzzle. She was going to do her puzzle just like her grandmother wasn't there.

It wasn't right. In fact, it was downright mean. I gathered what little was left of my patience (I'd completely run out of understanding) and suggested, "Valerie, you should show your grandmother around. The fireplaces and paneling and stuff are like in those stately houses they have in England. It'd make her feel at home."

"Not now." And she fitted the piece into the puzzle.

Gran's face looked like Valerie'd slapped it. I couldn't bear to see her so hurt. I turned away.

Then something strange happened to me. It was like I was walking in the street with Mama and some punk stopped us and beat Mama up right in front of my eyes. I got this buzzing in my head and this boiling feeling in my chest like there was a volcano inside of me about to explode.

I tried to hold it back. Really I did. But the words poured out from between my clenched teeth. "Valerie, you're a selfish witch. You think because something terrible happened to you, it gives you the right to wipe your feet on other people. You act like nobody has feelings but you. We're all standing on our heads to do things for you, and you treat us like we don't exist. Well, I have news for you. Your grandmother has feelings. Your mother has feelings. I have feelings. And if you don't care about us, you can stay in this place for the rest of your life enjoying your misery, and we won't lift one little finger to help you."

You won't believe what happened next. Valerie Ross,

the original temper tantrum kid, Valerie, who'd curse out the pope if he crossed her, just smiled and went on doing her puzzle. Then I, Teresa D'Angelo, who's spent her whole life being a good girl, took out my fury on the vase with Marc's rose floating around in all that water. I shoved the vase straight at Valerie!

The rest happened fast, but I saw it in slow motion like a TV sports replay. The vase slid into the puzzle, scattering the pieces. Then it toppled over and the water spurted out like when you turn on the shower. Valerie was drenched. Water dripped from her hair, turned her sweatshirt into a soggy mess, and puddled in her lap.

For a long slow-motion moment, Valerie sat in the water. I couldn't move, either. I was too shocked by what I'd done.

Then, grabbing the edge of the table, she pulled herself to her feet. She walked out of the worst of the wet and stood there, with her hands braced on the table for support, shaking the water off herself like a puppy.

I was the first one to realize it. "Valerie! You're standing!"

Then Amanda and Gran saw it too. Amanda cried, "Your good leg is working. It's holding you."

Gran whispered, "Thank God."

Valerie let herself down onto a dry chair. She stared at her leg and smiled like she knew some joke we didn't. "The doctors have been saying all along it was in my head. I guess they were right. Who'd've thunk it?" Then she started to cry.

Valerie once bragged to me that she never cries. Now she made up for lost time. She didn't just cry. She burst into a flood of tears. If she wasn't wet already, her tears would've drenched her. She sobbed her heart out, not caring that everyone in the room was staring at her. She howled like an animal with its leg caught in a trap.

A nurse came running to stop the disturbance. Amanda put her hand on the nurse's arm. "Please. Let her cry. It's been too long coming."

I wanted to put my arms around Valerie and comfort her, but I knew Amanda was right. So I stood there, with my own eyes filling with tears, and watched Valerie mourn.

When the storm was almost over, I whispered to Amanda, "She'll be all right now, won't she?"

"I think so. I hope so."

28

Teri

———

Two Years Later

I came up from the mailbox clutching the envelope in my sweaty hand, trying to work up the nerve to open it. My fate for the next four years—maybe for my whole life—depended on the letter inside. If it said yes, I'd be doing something that no girl I knew ever did before, something that nobody in the family ever heard of a girl doing, something I was scared I wasn't smart enough or dedicated enough to do. If it was a no . . . Funny, I hadn't given any thought to what I'd do if they turned me down.

Little Tony heard me open the apartment door and came running for me to swing him in the air. He loves to be swung, bounced, or thrown—the harder the better. He's a little perpetual motion machine. Sometimes he's a pest, but I can't imagine the world without him. It'd be so quiet and dull. I gave him a good swing.

"More!"

"Later. I have to read this now." I opened the envelope. My hands were shaking and my heart was banging like it was going to jump out of my chest.

"Read to Tony."

I read out loud, "Dear Ms. D'Angelo. We are pleased to . . ." I screamed. He thought it was a game and screamed too. Mama and Rosanne came running to see what happened. Waving the letter wildly, I yelled, "I made it! They want me! I got accepted into the engineering program at City!"

You've never seen such telephoning. Mama ran to call Papa at the garage—even though she never bothers him at work except for a real emergency. Then she called Aunt Paula, who'd never forgive us if she wasn't told first. Then Aunt Flo and Aunt Sophie. Aunt Flo asked to talk to me personally to tell me how proud she was. Next on Mama's list was Mrs. Nicolosi, who could be counted on to spread the news through the whole building by morning. Meanwhile, Aunt Flo must've done some phoning of her own because the second Mama hung up to finish making supper, the phone rang and it was Marc saying he always knew his favorite cousin had a good brain in her pretty little head. I was glad Marc couldn't see my face because I always blush when he flirts with me like I was his girlfriend.

Then Papa was home and wanted to see the letter. Then it was suppertime. So I waited to call Peter till the dishes were done, Mama went to put Little Tony to bed, Papa took the paper into the living room, Rosanne went to wash her hair, and I was able to use the kitchen phone in private. Rosanne and I are after Papa for a phone in our room, but so far, no luck.

Of course, Rosanne came in looking for lemon juice for her hair just as Peter answered.

Peter was real happy for me. He told me I'd made his day. Then he asked, "Are you scared?"

"How'd you know?"

"When Columbia accepted me, I was terrified I wouldn't measure up. But after Sister Josephine, everything else, including college, is easy. Don't worry. You'll do fine."

"I hope so."

"I'll take you someplace special Saturday to celebrate."

Hoping the special someplace wasn't a science lecture, I said, "Great. See you Saturday."

When I hung up, Rosanne—who, of course, was listening—commented, "You and Peter have the least romantic conversations of any couple I know."

I answered, "Dear Abby had a column about people who listen in on other people's private conversations. She says it's the height of rudeness."

"Pardon me for living." She started shoving things around in the refrigerator, searching for a lemon. When Rosanne stops being neat, it means she's upset.

I always feel guilty when I hurt someone's feelings. "I didn't mean to snap at you. I just get tired of you always being my big sister. I'll be going to college next fall. It's time you stopped watching over me."

"I should hope so. You can't expect me to take care of you all your life." She made it sound like it was my fault she bossed me around.

It was on the tip of my tongue to say I'd take care of myself just fine if she'd stop butting into my business, but I didn't want to make it into a big deal. I get mad more than I used to, but I'll still walk around the block to avoid a fight. I changed the subject. "I think I'll call Valerie and tell her the news."

"Valerie? But you haven't heard from her in ages. I wouldn't think you'd want to call her after the way she dropped you. All those Saturdays you took that long, cold trip to Sweetwater. Then, when she came home and didn't need you anymore, she forgot you existed."

"I thought you just said you were going to stop telling me what to do."

She shrugged. "Call Valerie if you want. It just bothers me to see people take advantage of you."

"Valerie didn't take advantage of me. And she didn't drop me. We just drifted apart. When Valerie finally got out of Sweetwater she had doctor appointments and physical therapy and schoolwork to make up, and I was doing things with Julia and Patsy and then Peter started asking me out . . ."

"It wouldn't've killed her to call you once in a while."

"Sometimes people need each other, and other times they don't. I mean, after her accident, Valerie felt like it was more than just her leg that got paralyzed. It was like her whole self was destroyed. She needed a friend who truly believed her leg didn't matter. A friend who thought she was terrific—leg or no leg."

Rosanne looked surprised that I was able to figure that out without any psychology courses like the ones she took in her nursing program. She had to admit, "That sounds right." It was nice to know as much as Rosanne for a change. Then it occurred to me that when I studied engineering I'd know more than she does about a lot of things. It was a lovely thought.

179

She asked, "What did you need from Valerie?"

My mind went blank like it always does when somebody springs a question on me. Then the answer popped out of my mouth like it was sitting there waiting for someone to ask. "I needed her to show me that the world is a bigger place than I thought."

Rosanne gave me a funny look, but all she said was, "If you're going to call Valerie, I'll go wash my hair."

She headed for the bathroom. I got some pie from the fridge to fortify myself before I called. As I ate it, I thought, wouldn't it be funny if Valerie thought of me this very minute and the phone rang and it was her?

Of course, the phone didn't ring. And I don't know why I felt so shy about calling. I was acting as silly as Julia when she broke up with her boyfriend. If she spotted him in the hall at school, she ran to hide, but she talked about him day and night. Of course, Julia's friends all understood. When you lose a boyfriend, people expect you to feel miserable and mad and relieved all at once. But if you lose a girlfriend and you tell your other friends that you have all kinds of feelings about it, they think you're weird.

Without giving myself any more time to think, I picked up the receiver and dialed. As I counted the rings, I had the uncomfortable feeling that I'd dialed the wrong number. Maybe I'd forgotten. Maybe I should hang up and call information. But the familiar voice finally answered.

"Valerie," I said, "it's Teri. It's so long since we talked, I bet you didn't recognize my voice." Without giving her a chance to say of course she did and she'd been meaning to call me—without giving her a chance not to say it—I plunged right in, "I got this terrific news and I had to tell you."

I told her about getting accepted into the engineering program at City and how wonderful I felt, but that I was scared too, and that Peter told me that after Sister Josephine it'd be easy, and in a way Sister Josephine helped me get in, because when the petition worked I realized I could do all kinds of things I didn't think I could do before, and wasn't it great news?

Being Valerie, she said she wasn't surprised. "I always knew you could do it. It was just a matter of your having the confidence, and the petition gave it to you." Then she added, "Actually, the petition was fun."

At the time, I'd mostly been terrified. But come to think of it, Valerie was right. It had been fun too. I said, "We had a lot of fun together. Remember our birthday weekend? The party at my house and the brunch on the yacht?"

"Right." Then there was silence.

It's bad enough when you're talking to someone face-to-face and she gets all quiet. But at least you know she didn't go to the bathroom or something. I asked, "What about you? Where are you going to college?"

"Oxford."

"Oxford in England?"

"No, Oxford in Antarctica. I'm going to read English literature with the penguins."

I played it straight, like she expected me to. "Will you stay with your grandmother?"

"I'll be living at the college, but naturally I'll spend some weekends with Gran. We'll go to the theater and such."

Of course, Valerie would live at college and go to the theater and such. She always did special things. For a second, I wished I could go with her. Which was silly. I had my own life. I was going to study engineering at City. "I liked your grandmother. She sent me a card last Christmas."

When Valerie just said, "Um," I figured she didn't want to be reminded of the day I met her grandmother. I could understand that. It still embarrassed me to remember how I blew up. I never did anything like that before—or since. I asked, "How is your leg doing?"

"Which leg?"

I'd almost forgotten what talking to Valerie was like. But as she'd just said, I had more confidence now. "The right leg. The leg you hurt when you fell off the ladder. The other one was all in your head. Remember?"

"Well, well. You aren't as easy to tie into knots as you used to be." Strangely, she sounded pleased. "Actually, my leg is much better. Since it's more than two years since the accident, the doctors say I probably won't get much more return, but you never know. Anyway, my knee is working, so I got rid of the leg brace. Instead I wear a plastic gadget that fits under my foot and up the back of my calf. It's invisible under pants. And the crutches are long gone. They gave me a cane, but I refused to look like an old lady. I dropped the cane down the incinerator; it made a satisfying clatter as it fell. I'm working on getting rid of my limp so by the time I go to Oxford, nobody will be able to spot anything wrong with me. And I certainly won't tell them."

"Are you sure that's such a good idea? Maybe it'd be easier on you if . . ."

"I don't want them to know!" Then she was all news again. "Amanda is trying to get a transfer to the London office. She says she's homesick, and with Gran and me both in England, there's nothing to keep her here. If Amanda moves to London, I probably won't come back to New York again, either."

Why did I suddenly feel like somebody died? I hadn't seen Valerie for ages. What difference did it make if she was ten blocks or three thousand miles away? "Then I guess I won't see you again after you go to Oxford."

She didn't take the hint. She didn't say college didn't start till September so we had months to see each other before then. She didn't invite me over. But I thought she sounded sad when she said, "Ships passing in the night and all that jazz. Anyway, congratulations on the engineering."

I couldn't let it go like that. I had to tell her, "I owe it all to you. I'd never've dreamed of applying to engineering school if it wasn't for you."

There was a long silence. I steeled myself for a smart-aleck comeback. But she answered, "I'd probably still be in Sweetwater if it weren't for you, so we're even." Then, like she was embarrassed by what she'd just said, she laughed and added, "So build me a bridge. Bye." And she hung up.

I said into the dead phone, "Goodbye, Valerie. Be happy."

Rosanne came in, toweling her hair. "How's Valerie?"

"Her leg's doing better and she's going to college at Oxford in England. Do you know what I just realized? She didn't curse once the whole time we were talking."

"Maybe she's not so angry at the world anymore." Then

183

Rosanne reminded me, "Did you talk to Papa yet about going to the mountains with me this summer? If I were you, I'd nail him down while he's still excited about City accepting you."

"I'll do it now."

In the few steps between the kitchen and the living room, it hit me that working in the mountains is Rosanne's thing, not mine. Rosanne likes it because she gets to use the hotel facilities when she's off duty. But I'm not Rosanne. I don't care about swimming or tennis. And I don't really want to be a waitress.

I marched into the living room. "Papa," I began, before I could lose my nerve, "You know how busy you are at the garage in the summer and you hire a boy to help out and sometimes he doesn't know as much as he said he did. Well, what if you could hire an engineering student this summer? An engineering student who's good with her hands and eager to learn."

"And who might that be?"

"Me." I said it loud and clear.

"I only pay minimum wage."

"Papa! Do you mean it? Would you really give me the job?"

"How can I turn down an engineering student?"

As I threw my arms around Papa and hugged him, I thought, Valerie would be proud of me.